RUNNING FOR OUR LIVES

RUNNING FOR OUR LIVES

Glennette Tilley Turner

drawings by Samuel Byrd

Holiday House/New York

Library of Congress Cataloging-in-Publication Data
Turner, Glennette Tilley.
Running for our lives / Glennette Tilley Turner : drawings by
Samuel Byrd.—1st ed.
p.   cm.
Summary: A family of fugitive slaves becomes separated while
traveling to freedom aboard the Underground Railroad.
ISBN 0-8234-1121-4
[1. Fugitive slaves—Fiction.   2. Slavery—Fiction.
3. Underground railroad—Fiction.   4. Afro-Americans—Fiction.]
I. Byrd, Samuel, ill.   II. Title.
PZ7.T8547Ru   1994   93-28430   CIP   AC
[Fic]—dc20

To John G. Jackson, Sadie Warren, Ida Cress, Blanche and Brenda Elliott, and the Glenn and Tilley families

SPECIAL THANKS To Arlie Robbins, Mary Frances Shura, Ben Richardson, Bryan and Allen Walls of the John Freeman Walls Historic Site and Underground Railroad Museum, the North American Historical Museum, Charles L. Blockson, Darwin Walton, Stephen Richardson and Nayshon Mosley of the Project F.A.M.E. Upward Bound program, Carl Landrum, Marilyn Kayton, DuSable Museum, Mark Chapman, Off Campus Writers' Workshop, Marge Edwards, Ezby Collins, Jean Burger, Charlotte Johnson, Evelyn Johnson, Mary Hyndman, Juliet Walker, Margaret Dutton, Society of Children's Book Writers, Megan Degorski and Patricia Frontain, the reference librarians at Night Owl Reference Service, Wheaton Public Library, Glen Ellyn Public Library, Newberry Library, Quincy Public Library, Susan Warner and fellow staff members at Arrow Rock State Historic Site, Friends of Arrow Rock, Lois Conley, Simeon Osby, Ron Burleson, Father Thomas Hanlon, Mary Peccarelli, Carolyn Sexhauer, Virginia Julien, Valerie Kee, Patricia S. Robinson, Gruen and Les Primitif galleries, Chicago Historical Society, and the Illinois Michigan Canal Authority

Prologue

PLACE: *The Freeman family reunion, North Buxton, Ontario, Canada*
TIME: *Labor Day, September 1945*

This was the best part of the family reunion. Alicia, A.J., Adam, and their cousins gathered under the old apple tree to hear their great-grandpa tell about the true life adventures of his boyhood.

Alicia said, "Tell us about the secret cave you found."

A.J. added, "You know that's not the beginning of the story."

Adam chimed in, "Please start with when the trouble began."

Great-grandpa Luther tapped his ebony walking stick on the ground and leaned back in the cane chair beneath the apple tree. His words transported his great-grandchildren to another time and place as he began to tell their favorite family story.

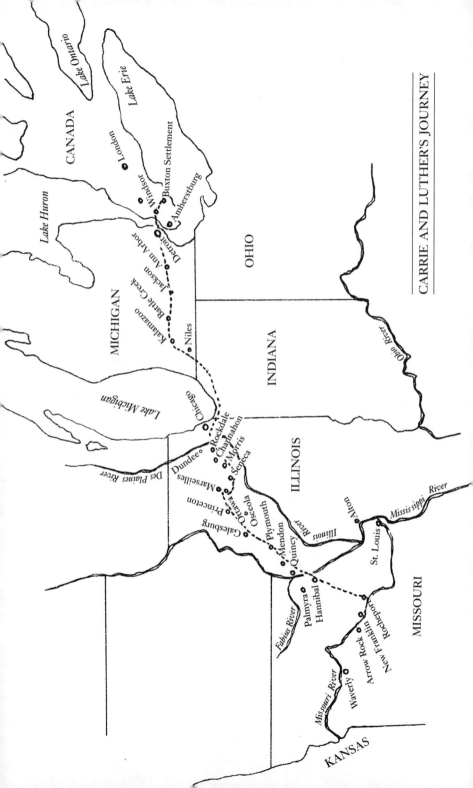

CARRIE AND LUTHER'S JOURNEY

RUNNING FOR
OUR LIVES

CHAPTER

I

I'd been groomin' horses for Cap'n for a year when the trouble came in the fall of 1855. It started low, like a summer storm growlin' along the western sky. But like those storms, it kept risin' until when I heard the shout.

"Luther, get yourself out here!"

I shot out of the stable. You couldn't say it "paid" you to move fast when Cap'n yelled 'cause there's no such thing as a slave bein' paid. But you could sure get the "business end" of Cap'n's whip if he thought you were draggin' your feet.

After the trouble started—between Missouri slaveholders like Cap'n and the antislavery people in Kansas—that shout always meant one thing. Cap'n was back with his great fine horse, Thunder, dogged from hard ridin'.

Cap'n dismounted. He handed me the reins and rushed around the stable to the house.

Nobody but me could groom Thunder without him putting up a fight. He was bigger than most horses by half a hand and broad across the chest. For all that, he could run like the wind.

When Cap'n brought him back from those raids, Thunder'd stand head down like a dray horse, his great lungs workin' like bellows fightin' for the wind to breathe. Ropy suds of foam would spill from his mouth and sweat would run off his broad rump like a waterfall. Sometimes he looked white around the eyes, like he was scared that one of his gaspin' breaths would be his last. Yet as much as I liked that horse, and as glad as I was to see him calm down as I groomed him, I felt with every stroke of my brush I was helpin' Cap'n tighten the bonds around my own family.

We were stuck—me, Mama, Carrie, and Dilly, the knee-high baby we'd taken in when her own mother was sold to another owner—on this planta-tion near New Franklin, Missouri. Our daddy was a coachman over in Waverly, where he'd been sold by our master a year ago.

Just as I was thinkin' 'bout Daddy, I heard the sound of wheels comin' along the road. Sure enough, it was a carriage.

I didn't want to get my hopes up. It could be any one of Cap'n's cronies, but I sure wished it would be my daddy bringin' his master for a visit. If it was, I could see Daddy and tell him 'bout the escape cave I'd found.

"Escape" was a word no slave dared to say out loud. Once when I was little, I'd heard some other children whisperin' about it. I asked Mama what did it mean.

"Shhh!" Mama had said. "Escape? That's just a lovely dream, Luther."

Even though I was young, I knew I didn't like bein' somebody's property, like a horse or a cow. And 'most everything starts with a dream. So I held on to the dream that someday our family could escape. The cave I'd found seemed like our one big chance.

The closer the carriage got, the more my hopes grew. Finally the carriage was close enough for me to see who was drivin' it. It was my daddy!

My heart was poundin' as I stood near the waterin' trough, tryin' to calm Thunder. I knew Daddy would bring his horses around to drink, like all the other coachmen, and maybe we could whisper then.

How I wished I was free. Then I could run up to greet Daddy. Just the thought of that got me daydreamin' about how it'd be if our whole family was free. We could live together all the time and come and go as we pleased. But this kind of dreamin' was silly. You can't go actin' free when you're a slave. Let me once run to greet Daddy, and I know Cap'n would whip the daylights out of me, and maybe sell me to a place so far away I could never find my family again.

It seemed to take Daddy a long time to take his master to the front of the big house, then pull around by the stable. I knew he didn't want to act too anxious either.

I wondered if his heart was thumpin' like mine. Ever since I heard that he was a coachman, I'd been hopin' he'd get a chance to bring his master over to our place. Now he was comin'.

Daddy unhitched his horses and brought them over to the waterin' trough. Speakin' in such a way that his lips hardly moved, Daddy said, " 'Ello, Luther. How you-all doin'?"

I tried to answer without movin' my lips either. "Fine."

"Keep your head turned while we talk, but listen," ordered Daddy. "Tell your mama things lookin' pretty bad over to my new place."

"Here, too, Daddy. I'll tell her what you said."

He looked toward the big house. "I sure wish I could step into that kitchen to see her—and tell her my own self."

Knowin' we didn't have much time, I hurried and told Daddy, "Mama said she heard Cap'n say he and

some other masters been all up and down the river scarin' folks who want Kansas to be free. I knowed he'd been somewhere far—by the way he rode this poor horse."

Daddy patted his horses as if he was talkin' to them. Instead he was tellin' me, "They're plannin' something now, judgin' by the way my master ran into the house. Maybe Mama can hear them talk while she's servin' their dinner."

I blurted out, "Daddy, I found us a cave—over near Rocheport. If we could all get that far . . ."

Daddy looked toward the big house again. "Shhh! Got to go now."

As I watched him leave, I could hardly wait till nighttime to tell Mama what he had said.

I was sure glad when all my chores were done. As I got to our log cabin, I thought, Carrie will be through in the smokehouse, and Mama will be comin' in with scraps from the kitchen.

Instead, it was a good while before either one of them got home.

When I did hear someone comin', I looked out through the cracks between the logs. Neither Mama nor Carrie was in sight. Mama's friend, Liz, was walkin' past.

I looked at the inside of our little cabin. All that was in it was a table made with two barrels and a plank. And two beds made of straw and old rags.

Before he was sold Daddy had boxed in the beds with boards. That way the blankets didn't soak up as much mud from the floor. Mama had told us about wood floors and fancy furniture at the big house. Daddy had heard some houses were even finer than that. But this was the only home I'd ever known.

Someone else was comin'. This time it was Carrie and the baby. Mama wasn't far behind them, with leftovers and news from the big noon meal.

"Mama, did you see Daddy while he was here today?" I began.

Wearily she said, "No, son, I was goin' back and forth between the hot kitchen and the dinin' room."

I went on: "Well, as Daddy watered his horses, he said to tell you things lookin' bad over to his place. I told him same here."

Mama said, "From the way the masters were talkin', things soon goin' to be even worse. While servin' them dinner, I overheard Daddy's master say, 'We slaveholders have to stick together. If we don't, John Brown and the abolitionists will get Kansas in the Union as a Free State!' He made it sound like that was the worst thing that could ever happen."

Carrie and I leaned forward as Mama almost whispered, "Those planters are jumpy as squirrels. They so worried about losin' their slaves, they might do *anything!*"

"Anything?" I asked.

Mama said, "Yes. Why, when the missus asked Cap'n if he'd even go so far as to break the law, he answered her, 'Yes, ma'am. We'll make our own law. We'll stuff ballot boxes and do whatever else is necessary to keep our slaves!' "

"I always knew he was a hard man," said Carrie. "Remember when their daughter, Susan, used to teach me to read?"

"Yes, indeed," answered Mama. "I remember how awful he acted when he caught you readin' the Bible! Imagine that, makin' it into a crime to read the Bible, of all things!"

"Do *I* ever remember," Carrie said as she gingerly touched the lash mark on her back. "Readin' must set you free, judgin' by the way he ordered Susan *never* to teach *that* to a slave! What he doesn't know is I remember everything she ever taught me, plus I figured out some other things for myself."

Mama said, "Cap'n wasn't fair to you or his daughter, but in a way I know why he acted like that. Both him and Missus started out poor. Cap'n's daddy was a straw boss on a Kentucky horse plantation. As a boy, Cap'n worked on a riverboat."

"Was that how he got the name Cap'n?" I asked.

"I bet he named himself that," Carrie figured.

Mama smiled and went on. "Seems like folks on the riverboat told him there was good land in Missouri. Missus's daddy was a poor dirt farmer, so this was just what they were lookin' for."

Carrie nodded. "Yeah, they saw how they could get themselves some slaves and live like the folks their folks used to work for."

"Is that when they bought you and Daddy?" I asked.

"Yes," Mama said.

"Where did they buy you?" Carrie asked.

"In the St. Louis slave market," Mama told her. "We heard there were some black men there who helped free slaves, but we'd just come from Virginia and didn't know how to find them."

"Couldn't you have asked somebody?" Carrie asked.

Mama explained: "Harvey Lee and I were just younguns. We'd been taken from our parents and were scared and homesick." She got real quiet, then smiled as she said, "I think that's why we took a likin' to each other."

I wanted to ask Mama questions about our grandparents, but she was still talkin'. "Let me tell you, Cap'n bought us and Liz and Matthew. They were a little older than your daddy and me. We all came to New Franklin on a boat from St. Louis, then built some log cabins. When we first got here we lived like one big family. But we always knew Cap'n was the boss."

"You and Daddy used to help with the farmin', didn't you, Mama?" asked Carrie.

She nodded. "Yes, we worked tobacco after we cleared the fields. Tobacco is why Cap'n wanted slaves from Virginia. He knew we knew what to do with tobacco."

"How'd you get to do the cookin'?" I knew the answer but I wanted to hear it again. I loved to hear Mama talk about the old days.

Mama explained: "Liz was a good cook, but when she had her baby, I had to take her place. Cap'n liked my sweet potato puddin'. That's how I got the job as Liz's helper. By that time Cap'n had brought in some more slaves to work in tobacco. I was still just fifteen or so."

Carrie asked, "What about Daddy? When'd you find out Daddy loved you, Mama?"

Mama smiled. "Every chance he got he'd be up at the big house pokin' around tryin' to see me. Oh, he was somethin' to look at! Liz used to tease me about gettin' all flustered whenever he came around. Finally she told me I was old enough to be thinkin' about gettin' hitched. Harvey Lee must have been thinkin' the same thing, 'cause one day he came up to me and said, 'Let's stop playin' hide-and-seek and tie the knot.'"

Carrie always asked about Mama and Daddy's love story. Mama looked like she was goin' to cry when she finished talkin'.

I changed the subject. "Daddy was still workin' tobacco in those days, wasn't he, Mama? I remember the day he started workin' with horses. Cap'n always rather be on his horse than anywhere else. When he used to come to the tobacco field, Cap'n would sit on that horse and tap his foot at the speed he thought the slaves ought to be workin'. If anybody so much as missed a lick at his work, he'd tell the overseer. 'Get the bullwhip ready,' he'd say."

"Luther, even though you're eleven and I'm ten, you're not the only one that remembers that. I remember, too," said Carrie.

"Your daddy would still be in the fields if Cap'n's horse hadn't been nipped by that bullwhip one day," Mama told us. "That horse was scared silly. It snorted and reared back and threatened to throw Cap'n to kingdom come."

"What happened then?" asked Carrie.

Mama sounded proud as she answered, "Your daddy just raised his hand and said, 'Whoa,' and that horse calmed down just as nice. Ever since then, your daddy's been known for his way with horses."

"I know Daddy was glad to get a chance to work with them," I told Mama.

"He was," said Mama, "but the word spread for miles around. Pretty soon a horse farmer from Waverly offered Cap'n so much money for Daddy that next thing we knew, your daddy was bein' sold."

I added, "Cap'n must not've thought about how Daddy must've felt leavin' us."

Mama finished, "Or how we felt havin' him leave."

This time Carrie was the one to change the subject. "They found out Luther was good with horses almost the same way they found out about Daddy."

"Yeah, except it was the overseer, not Cap'n, who noticed that I could say a little somethin' to the mule. Hardly anybody else could get that stubborn mule to pull the tobacco sled, even if they yelled at him," I said.

"Lucky you finally got to be a groom in the stable, or you wouldn't have got to see Daddy today," Carrie added.

I thought about that and looked at the sadness in Mama's eyes.

Mama shook her head and said, "Don't call it luck when there's not a thing we can do about gettin' our family back together."

Carrie stamped her foot. "There *has* to be!" she said. "And now there's troubles at Daddy's place and ours. We've got to try to escape before things get worse."

Mama grabbed Carrie's arm. "Hush, girl! Don't even joke like that!"

Carrie hugged Mama and stammered, "I didn't mean to be jokin'. Ma, things only goin' to get worse here."

Mama looked unhappy. "That's true, but we can't just hope to get away. Even if we could, I wouldn't leave without your daddy. It's bad enough he was sold way over to Waverly, but at least we can hope to see him once in a while, like Luther did today."

"Mama, I don't mean *leave* Daddy. Couldn't we make a plan with him, so we could escape together?" asked Carrie.

For a minute Mama's face lit up. "Lord, chile, I wish we could." She stood up and put her hands on her hips. "But I never have heard of a whole family gettin' away."

"We've all got to go," said Carrie.

"It's not that simple," said Mama. "Some one of us would be sure to get caught, then we'd be forced to tattle on the others." Almost angrily Mama explained, "We couldn't just walk off. Those slave catchers would soon be trackin' us down with their dogs. Even if we was to get away, them bloodhounds would smell our scent and find us. They would rip us to pieces. You hear me?"

Carrie squinched up her face.

I hadn't said a word while they were talkin'. Finally I whispered, "Mama, I found a cave over near Rocheport." Mama shuddered with fright. "I didn't say nothin' about this before, 'cause I thought you'd fuss, but one day when I was exercisin' that new thoroughbred, I stumbled—or really, he stumbled—in a sinkhole. It felt like there was a cool breeze blowin' out of it. I hitched the horse a good ways from there, then took the tether rope I used to stake him. I tied one end to the horse, held the other end, and let myself down into the hole. After you get down there and walk a while, it gets pitch dark. Holdin' onto my rope, I felt my way along. Pretty soon, I saw a speck of daylight. I had to wade through some water to get to the light, but I found a way out of the cave. It brought you out in some woods."

Carrie looked like she was about to jump out of her skin. She shook my arm. "Boy, why didn't you say somethin' sooner?" Then she turned to Mama. "Mama, I think he's makin' that up."

"I am not!" I said. "I thought Mama'd say I was crazy to get my hopes up. But now it looks like somethin' bad is 'bout to happen whether we stay or go."

The minute I stopped talkin', Carrie put her arm around Mama's shoulder and begged, "Oh, Mama, can we be ready just in case we get a chance to escape? Can we?"

Mama said, "Stop right there! It's against my better judgment to even think about makin' an escape plan. Nine chances out of ten we would get caught, and if they catch you they whip you till you bleed, then soak your cuts in pickle juice."

"I know it's dangerous, Mama, but can't we stash

some stuff in Luther's cave? Please, Mama, please!"
Carrie pleaded.

Mama finally said, "Oh, all right, children, I guess
you got to have a dream. But everything must be
kept secret, I do mean everything, just in case we
can work out something with your daddy."

The next few weeks, Carrie and I tried not to
hum or sing or do anything that would get anyone
suspicious, but we were like two happy little ants,
storin' our secret stash. We saved biscuits and apples
and every scrap of food that wouldn't spoil, includin' ham scraps Mama'd brought home. Carrie
saved dry bread left over from feedin' the chickens
and I found some pieces of flint for makin' a fire. We
also stashed a blanket. Mama just shook her head
and smiled, sayin', "Bless you, my children." Even
the baby Dilly seemed calmer and quieter, as if she
sensed our new hope.

Mama saw how this kept us goin'. I knew she
thought it was hopeless, but as a mother, she
couldn't bring herself to dash our hopes. What we
didn't know was that she had hidden some things for
the journey, too.

Everything seemed to be movin' along well, until
toward the end of November—the twenty-third to
be exact—when new things began to happen. The
fuss between the Missouri planters and Kansas set-
tlers was gettin' worse. Mama came home sayin' at

dinner that night Cap'n had told his wife, "A pro-slavery man killed a free soil man." A few nights later he was fumin' mad when he told Missus, "Those dirty free soldiers burned two of our men's cabins!" Missus asked him, "Was anybody hurt?" Cap'n looked embarrassed and mumbled, "Actually, no. The cabins were empty, but still . . ."

Two days after Thanksgivin', I saw a man racin' his horse toward the big house. As he got closer, I saw that he was a black man, and minutes later, I saw that it was my daddy! He and the horse were all wet and splattered with mud. He must have swum across the dangerous Missouri River. He ran to the front door, wavin' something in his hand.

I wasn't the only one who had seen him or who was wonderin' what in the world had happened. Every slave on the place stopped work to look. The overseers were so busy watchin' him, they didn't even notice we'd quit for a moment.

Inside the big house, Daddy was deliverin' a message his master had sent. It was callin' all the slave-holders to arms to fight the abolitionists in Kansas.

Finally, after the longest kind of time, Daddy brought the horse around to the waterin' trough. He looked much older than he had just a month before. His horse was pantin' and foamin' even worse than Cap'n's horse ever did. Something had to be awful wrong for Daddy to treat a horse like that!

Daddy's first words were, "Give me a fresh horse and listen quick. Your master's ridin' with me!"

Just then Cap'n yelled out the back door, "Get my horses ready. I'm going to *WAR!*"

My mouth must have dropped open, 'cause Daddy said, "Close your mouth and listen quick. I'll be back here midnight tomorrow, or never. Either way, you four at least try to escape. I love you all." Then he tucked something into the palm of my hand. It was a tiny gold statue of a man on horseback. For a long wonderful minute, Daddy closed his two big hands around my hand. He looked at me, then he looked at the little statue. "This is an Ashanti gold weight. It's the only thing my daddy, your granddaddy, brought from Africa. He called it a mramnuo. And he had to hide it. It's yours to keep." Whirlin' his horse around, he said, "Goodbye, and God bless you, my son."

Quickly an army of slaveholders rode off behind Daddy. I clutched the tiny statue as I looked at the real live men on horseback.

CHAPTER

2

The next day, it seemed like we'd been waitin' an endless time to leave Cap'n and New Franklin, Missouri, forever.

No tellin' how long Cap'n would be gone. Sometimes when the planters and Border Ruffians rode on Kansas, they'd get chased right back across the river. Sometimes they'd make camp for several days. With all the excitement, something bad was brewin' over there. When those planters came back there was goin' to be terrible trouble. People in the slave quarters feared they'd be whipped or sold. They dreaded the planters' return.

Realizin' the danger, many slaves started off, not

knowin' where to look for safety, but feelin' sure things would soon be much worse here.

Carrie and I watched as others left the previous night. Liz and her husband were so anxious they took off without anywhere to go. They chanced gettin' themselves caught and that made it more dangerous for our family.

We were feelin' more and more nervous. Other slave families were gettin' ready to leave. Some told us whispered good-byes.

Would the master return at noon? At suppertime? In the night?

I begged, "Mama, Mama, can we leave soon as it's dark?"

Mama reminded me, "You know what your daddy said, boy!"

"I'm sorry to keep worryin' you, Mama, but midnight may be too late."

"I know you're worried, son. So am I, but we just got to take this chance."

Later Daddy told us what chances he'd been takin' since we'd seen him ride away. He had to ride back toward Waverly 'cause so many angry planters were headed in that direction on their way to Kansas. If he had tried to double back to our family's place, the planters were in such a mood, they might have tried to lynch him.

Daddy and the planters were travelin' on the

Santa Fe Trail. They rode from New Franklin and crossed the Missouri River on the ferry at Arrow Rock. Although they stopped long enough to water their horses at Big Spring, they pressed on down the trail to Neff's Tavern before they stopped for the night. Bein' a slave, Daddy wasn't given a place to stay inside the tavern. Instead, he was expected to sleep in the hayloft of the barn.

He waited until the middle of the night when he was quite sure all the angry planters were sound asleep. He couldn't risk takin' his horse from the barn, so he started walkin' back to our place. His only tool was an ax he had found and buried just in case he might have need for it.

Daddy was obliged to make his way through miles of mud, bramble bushes, briar patches, deep forests, and rocky hills. He inched his way back to Arrow Rock.

Arrow Rock had been an Indian meetin' place where many tribes had come to get flint for their arrows. An old East-West trail crossed the Missouri River there.

Daddy was familiar with Arrow Rock, since he had brought his new master to its saddlery. While the master had gone to the front of the shop, orderin' saddles and harnesses and such, Daddy had gone in back and talked with a slave who worked at the saddlery. Daddy said he learned a lot of helpful things from that man—includin' how to reach the river without bein' seen by people workin' on the riverfront.

Now Daddy crept down to the spring to get fresh water. He found a log and some branches to use as poles and an out-of-the way spot in the bottomland where he could rest. He hid there the next day, even though he was in a hurry. Daytime travel was too risky. From his hidin' place he could see the ferry-boat plyin' back and forth across the river and eagles flyin' free overhead.

He was in Arrow Rock waitin' for nightfall at the very minute that I was askin', "Mama, Mama, can we leave as soon as it's dark?"

Bein' winter, it got dark early in the evenin'. Daddy started out as soon as he dared. He followed the path the man at the saddlery had told him about. He headed for the treacherous Missouri River. There were so many tales about ships and crews and passengers goin' down, it was frightenin' to even think of a person swimmin' the river. But that was the only way Daddy dared cross it. He couldn't chance tryin' to stow on board the ferryboat.

Usin' poles, he pushed off into the current. He fought to stay clear of whirlpools and floatin' logs. He hadn't swum far before the river got too deep for the poles to touch bottom.

He ended up layin' on a log and usin' his arms and

legs to guide himself through the fast-movin', icy waters. He and the horse might have gotten splattered when he crossed the river last time, but it was much harder this way. Finally, he reached the other side and scrambled out, wet and cold, onto the riverbank. He couldn't rest long, though. Wearily he forced himself to keep goin'. Although the river had taken him about a half mile downstream he still had several more miles to travel before reachin' New Franklin. And he'd told us to leave if he wasn't there by midnight. For the next few hours he strained on so he could reach us. He arrived just as we were bundlin' the baby up to leave. He stood shiverin' at the side of the house where he wouldn't be seen and whispered, "It's me."

Carrie and I eased open the door. When I touched Daddy's arm, I realized his clothes were soppin' wet. So as Mama and Carrie greeted Daddy, I hurried to get him some dry clothes and food. We moved without a sound in that pitch-dark cabin, to do all the last-minute things. We'd miss our old home but it was time to leave now. One by one, we crouched and crept toward the woods. Although Cap'n and a lot of the other men-folk on the plantation were gone, they'd left blood-hounds behind, and Missus was so nervous that she kept a loaded shotgun.

Once in the woods, Carrie and I led the way toward my cave. We tried to tell Daddy about it, but he said, "Hush, I'll see it."

Dilly had been sleepin' peacefully in Daddy's arms. Being one and a half she was too little to walk fast enough to keep up. When Daddy shifted her weight, she woke up cryin'. Carrie and I could have cried, too; after *all* our plans and hope and work the baby's noise would spoil everything! Everyone froze, fearin' the worst.

Mama reached in her pocket and took out something she had fixed when we were plannin' our escape. It was a lump of sugar in a little sack, called a sugar tit. Mama poked it in Dilly's mouth. Dilly stopped cryin' as soon as she tasted the sweetness of the sugar. Pretty soon she went back to sleep. Whew!

CHAPTER

3

Moments after we began our escape, it was hard to feel free or even think of anything except gettin' off that plantation.

We didn't say a word as we walked toward the cave. The night was cold, but each of us was feelin' a glow inside. It was an excitement we'd never felt before. We'd always heard you should escape on a moonless night. But we got our chance on a night when the moon was bright, so we had to move like shadows.

I was wonderin' which cave entrance we should use. The one in the woods was the largest. It would be the easiest and softest for Mama and for Daddy with the baby in his arms, but if the bloodhounds followed our scent, the slave catchers could walk right in. Much as we'd dreamed of escapin', it's funny, Carrie and I had never talked about which entrance to use to get in the cave.

I led the way to the sinkhole. I tied some rope to a tree stump and climbed down. Mama's polished cookin' knife reflected enough moonlight for the rest of the family to see how deep they had to go. I held the rope taut. Carrie scurried down after me. She whispered, "I'll hold the knife. You steady the rope for Mama."

Mama came down cautiously, then reached her arms out as Daddy handed the baby to her. She checked her footin' as she stepped back a bit. Then Daddy climbed down. I should have gone back and untied the rope from the stump right then, but I was too anxious to show the others where to sleep.

I told the family what I'd found out about the cave, and which rough spots to watch for. Then I looped the middle part of my rope around an icicle-shaped stone near where we'd entered. I tied the free end to another stone in the cave, near a chamber where the family could settle for the rest of the night. They followed the rope to the chamber. Then once they were there, I hurried back to the sinkhole and climbed up to untie the rope from the stump. After I did that, I had to jump down into the sink-

hole without the rope to steady me. I landed on a rock and twisted my ankle. Even though the pain was terrible, I didn't tell anyone. I knew my parents would worry if they thought I was hurt. I coiled my rope around a solid rock that seemed to drip from the ceilin', then made my way to where the rest of the family was.

"It sure is scary in this cave," said Carrie. "Scary and fun at the same time. I wouldn't be surprised if we found rattlesnakes sleepin' in here."

"We'll sure try not to disturb 'em," said Mama.

I had something besides rattlesnakes to worry about. My ankle was hurtin' something awful.

"It's nice and warm in here. Warmer than that cabin ever was," said Mama.

Daddy teased, "*Was!* Listen to you, talkin' like a free woman already!" He hugged her, and in a more serious voice added, "I hope you will always be *free.*" When he said "free," there were tears in his voice.

I was too pleased with myself to sleep, but everyone else soon drifted off.

Sittin' in the darkness, I thought to myself, If it hadn't been for my underground cave, we would still be walkin'. Then I thought ahead, wonderin' what tomorrow and the rest of the future held.

I heard a sound.

Had I dozed off? Was I just imaginin' things?

No. There it was again.

This was something I hadn't expected. I'd thought of bein' hunted by men and dogs, and travelin' through bad weather, but this sound . . . It didn't sound like the rattlesnakes Carrie had talked about. It was a *whish, shish, whish* sound. And it was bein' made by something flappin' over my head!

I was so frightened I didn't know what to do. I don't know how long I sat there tremblin' before Daddy woke up. He scared the stew out of me when he said, "Luther, you 'wake, son?"

"Yeah, yeah, yessir," I finally stammered. "Do you hear that sound, Daddy?"

"It sounds like bats," he said.

"Bats," I repeated.

Daddy must have sensed how scared I was. "Don't be worried about those bats, son. They can fly around forever without strikin' you. They were sleepin' here for the winter, and we disturbed 'em."

"They sure had me scared," I said. "I never heard 'em when I was in the cave before."

Daddy put his strong arm around my shoulder. It made me feel everything was goin' to be all right.

"You know, when I was a boy, we used to catch big brown bats," he said.

"Were you scared?" I asked.

"No," he answered. "They're helpless while they hang upside down sleepin'. If you take 'em on the cave floor, they stretch, roll over on their backs, and fuss. Pretty soon they start to shiver. Next thing you know, they fly." Rubbin' his hands together to warm them, he said, "It's different in the summer. You have to catch 'em when they just begin flyin'. Used to catch 'em in little cages and feed 'em mealworms."

"Did you keep them, Daddy?" I asked.

"No, son. The first time I caught one, I kept it so that I could have at least one thing that really belonged to me. Then I thought, He wants to be free— just like me! So, I let him go. You should have seen that bat flap his wings!" Then he said, "We got a long hike tomorrow. I'll take this watch while you get some sleep." I felt happy as I dozed off with Daddy's arm around my shoulder. That was the way our first night ended. Our family was together again. At least for the time bein' we were safe. We'd made a break for our freedom, but we didn't know what lay ahead.

After Daddy's watch, Mama and Carrie took turns bein' the lookouts. It seemed like the middle of the night when they shook me. Everybody else was already awake. They'd let me sleep till the last minute.

We gulped down some ham scraps Mama had brought and some dry bread Carrie had saved.

We climbed out the cave openin' that was in the woods. It was still dark. Outside, the moon and most stars were hidden by clouds, but we could see the North Star shinin' through.

Slaves on the plantation said that the North Star could lead you to freedom in Canada, wherever that was. We were goin' to try to follow it. Not only could we see the North Star, the whole sky was jet black beautiful. It hid us as we walked between the tree trunks.

In the distance, we could hear hound dogs barkin'.

4

By early Tuesday mornin', on December 3, 1855, we had made it to a forest miles from Cap'n's plantation. We didn't know whether or not we'd been missed yet.

Daddy said, "I wonder if they tracked me to the Missouri River?"

Mama said, "Missus will soon know we left. This is about the time I start the kitchen fires each mornin'. Won't the missus be surprised to get up lookin' for me to serve hot breakfast and find I'm not there!"

"How long do you think it'll be before she sends somebody out lookin' for us?" asked Carrie.

"Well, it depends on who she sends," Mama answered. "Since her menfolk are all gone, she'll have to send a slave. If he's kindly he'll take his time and make out like he can't find no slave catchers to send after us. If he's tryin' to please the missus, he'll sick the posse on us right away. Whenever they come, the bloodhounds will lead them to the cave. It's good the dogs can't climb through that hole we went in."

"Another thing," Carrie said. "Our cave has so many tunnel rooms those slave catchers will waste a lot of time lookin' around in there."

"Maybe they'll even get lost," I added.

"Or maybe they'll find out where we got out," suggested Carrie.

"Sooner or later they most likely will," said Daddy.

"Anyways, we got a good head start," said Mama. "We must have gone miles by now."

She and Daddy and Carrie were leadin' the way, with me behind.

My ankle was still painin' me from the night before. I hoped I could walk without limpin'.

At first we had tried to hold the baby by the hand and let her walk, but you know how babies can pull back when you want 'em to hurry up, so we took turns carryin' her.

Darkness seemed to last extra long, like it was tryin' as best it could to protect us. It stayed cloudy even after daybreak, so it would have been hard for slave catchers to spot us movin' among the trees.

If we hadn't been runnin' for our lives, it would have been like a nice hike for our family. Every twig that snapped or forest animal that ran by made us stop still and freeze until we were sure of what made the sound.

Even so we couldn't help but notice how pretty the tall oaks were, how much their leaves looked like fingers, and how many acorns were on the ground. Daddy said these acorns could be used as food. He said he'd learned about things like that from my granddaddy who got interested in plants when he was a boy in Africa.

With every mile we walked, our hope of gettin' away grew a little. We all moved without a sound, but I knew each of us had a happy song in our hearts. When we got hungry, we nibbled on dried apple rings and pumpkin seeds that Mama had brought so we could keep goin'.

We were makin' such good speed that at almost the same time, Carrie and I asked, "How do we know we're goin' the right way?" It would have been horrible if we'd been headin' south, back toward the plantation, since durin' the day, there was no North Star to follow.

Daddy reminded us, "Moss grows on the north side of the tree." Of course. Ever since we were little, he'd told us, "Moss grows on the north side of the tree and rivers usually flow south." There was another way Daddy had taught us to figure out which way was north. Since the sun rises in the east and sets in the west, our shadow would be on our left side in the mornin' if we were facin' north, and on our right in the afternoon.

We pushed on through the woods, until judgin' by the sky, it was about four o'clock in the afternoon. The trees were gettin' smaller and farther apart. It looked like we were almost out of the woods, and since none of us had been this far away from the plantation before, we didn't know just what to expect.

Mama said, "It looks like we're about to come to a clearin' where we will be easy to see. Do you think we should spend the night here?"

"It's hard to know what to do," answered Daddy. "There are three or four more hours of daylight. But if we go through a clearin', the slave catchers can see us a mile away."

Mama, who'd been carryin' Dilly, continued: "And we have no way of knowin' if there are plantations or slave catchers nearby. We need to decide something soon. These woods are gettin' mighty sparse."

We walked on until we were at the edge of the clearin'. Mama turned to me and said, "Here, Luther, you carry this baby. You've been kind of slow reachin' for her all day."

That was true. It had been all I could do to keep from limpin' as I carried my own weight.

At first I took Dilly in my arms, then I thought it might be easier if I let her ride piggyback. She always liked that. I put her down and bent over so she could climb on my back. Well, instead of climbin' on my back, Dilly dashed off into the clearin', gigglin' and runnin' as fast as she could.

I scrambled to my feet. I forgot all about how we needed to be quiet. I yelled, "DILLY!"

You know how Mama, Daddy, and Carrie must have felt when they heard me yell and saw Dilly runnin' across that field in broad daylight!

At first we all tried to run hunched over, hopin' to be hidden in grasses in the clearin', but Dilly was gettin' farther and farther away.

CHAPTER

5

Bad ankle or not, I had to get Dilly. I'd put all of us in danger—first by lettin' her run away, then by yellin'. Even catchin' her wouldn't solve all the problems I'd caused. I told the rest of the family, "You-all crouch in the woods, so if I'm caught you still have a chance."

I bolted in the direction Dilly had gone. But I couldn't see or hear her anywhere. Soon I figured out why. She'd found a stream and was down on her hands and knees lookin' at her reflection in the water. I sure was glad to see that baby! I tiptoed up behind her for fear she'd run away again. I slid my arm around her shoulder and whispered, "Dilly, it's me." Instead of runnin', she just pointed at her reflection in the water, sayin', "See me!" Rather than start back to the rest of the family, I decided we should hide in a clump of bushes until dark. I held tight to Dilly this time, and she didn't like that one bit. She squirmed and kicked and cried until she finally fell asleep. I was relieved she hadn't gotten away again and that her cries hadn't led the slave catchers to us.

It seemed like a waste of time to be just sittin', but it was the safest thing to do. While waitin' in the bushes, I started thinkin' about Dilly's stream. Back on the plantation, whenever slaves whispered anything about escapin', they'd say, "Hound dogs lose your scent if you walk in water."

As soon as it was dark, I picked Dilly up in my arms. Luck was with us that she didn't wake up as I crept back to find Mama, Daddy, and Carrie. They were near where I'd left them. They were crouched in a place where they could see the outline of anyone walkin' toward them. They were glad to see Dilly and me safe and sound. When I told them about Dilly's stream, Mama said, "The Lord works in mysterious ways."

"Let's walk south in the stream," suggested Carrie.

"Girl, you're crazy," I said. "We got to get north as fast as we can. Why are you talkin' 'bout goin' south?"

"Think about it, Luther. Which way will the slave hunters expect us to go?" asked Carrie.

As soon as I answered "North," I realized what Carrie was thinkin'. After the slave catchers lost our scent, they'd take the dogs upstream tryin' to pick up our trail.

I said, "So if we go south, we can trick 'em, huh?"

She smiled and said, "Right."

In the moonlight we could see Mama and Daddy smilin' at us. Mama gently took Dilly out of my arms and said, "Luther, I want to look at your ankle as soon as we settle in for the night. I noticed you limpin' across that clearin'."

Daddy had been checkin' to make sure we weren't forgettin' anything. "Everybody ready?" he asked.

Carrie said, "Let's go."

We moved ever so slowly across the clearin'. Before long a cloud covered the moon, and we were able to stand up and walk a little faster. When we got to the stream, we stepped into the water right where I'd found Dilly. The scent we left at that spot and on the nearby bushes would really make the hounds think they were hot on our trail.

But we went south. The water was cold. Even so we knew the longer we could stay in it, the better.

We all complained about our cold feet. We'd taken off our flimsy shoes so they'd be dry when we got out of the water. As I dried my feet once we stopped, I realized my ankle wasn't swollen any-more. The cold water had been just what I'd needed.

Mama teased, "You're not goin' to need my doc-torin' after all."

From the stream we saw the dim outline of a clump of pine trees. We were cold and didn't want to go too much farther south. These woods seemed like a good place to spend the rest of the night. Dry pine needles covered the ground like a soft straw mat.

We went back a ways in the woods to find a good lookout point. Carrie had had a nap while she and Daddy and Mama were waitin' for Dilly and me, so she took the first watch. The family said I could sleep without takin' a watch that night.

I pulled one end of the blanket over me. The last thing I heard before I dozed off was Mama and Daddy talkin' as they dried their feet. Mama said, "Harvey Lee, wadin' in that water got me to won-derin'. Do we have to cross the Mississippi River?"

Daddy answered, "I'm not sure, Emma. But I swam across the Missouri last night when I was comin' to meet you-all. If we come to the Missis-sippi, we'll find some way to cross it, too."

Mama yawned and said, "You're right. No sense worryin' about that now."

When I opened my eyes the next mornin', I was lookin' up into the tall pines. I could just barely see the sky through the branches. It gave me the same feelin' as when you put your hands over your eyes and peek through your fingers. As the wind blew through the trees, they smelled good and had a kind of whisperin' sound. Everything was so peaceful here. Birds were flittin' around and a squirrel was prancin' from branch to branch with a pinecone in its mouth. It tried to act excited when it first saw us, but soon jumped to the ground and ran from place to place, hopin' to find a spot to bury the last of its winter food. It knew it had better hurry, 'cause the weather was already good and cold.

Daddy had been watchin' the squirrel and me. He said, "Did you know you can eat the seeds from these pinecones?"

"No, sir. Oh, good mornin'," I said when I saw everybody else up and ready to go.

Mama told me: "Luther, you can eat as we walk. Here's some ham and bread. And maybe you'd like to try some pine seeds."

I took the food she offered me, gathered up my things, and picked up a pinecone.

Daddy said, "I think any slave catchers who tracked us to the stream have given up by now. I think we should leave. It's probably safe to start walkin' north followin' the stream. We've got to be real careful, though, 'cause daytime travel is risky."

Our piney woods led to a forest of oak trees that were set back a ways from the stream. We walked through them for miles. Many of these oak trees had lost their leaves for winter. We didn't feel as well hidden by them. We could still see the stream in the distance.

We knew we must be near some plantations, since we could hear the faraway sound of cocks crowin'. Once we even saw slaves workin' with horses in the distance. At first I thought, That's the kind of work Daddy and I used to do. Then I thought, What do I mean, by "used to"? That was just the day before yesterday. It sure felt like it had been longer than that.

Daddy had different thoughts as we passed by those slaves. He said, "We better try to put a lot of distance behind us today. Escaped slaves make slaveholders uneasy. If the owner of this plantation was to capture us, he'd most likely be as hard on us as Cap'n."

Carrie whispered, "Look! There's an overseer ridin' his horse toward the field. What if he sees us?"

"Let's keep walkin' at the same pace but kind of sideways so we can get deeper into the woods," suggested Mama.

We went on. Walkin' in the woods was slow.

That night, Daddy said, "I think we best keep goin'. The moon is still pretty near full and if we walk at the edge of the forest we can make better time than walkin' between trees in the daytime. We

can step into the woods if we see somebody comin'."
Everybody liked Daddy's plan. We stopped just
long enough to eat before trudgin' on. Our supplies
were gettin' low, but we had enough for that night
and the next mornin'. I wondered out loud, "What
will we do when we run out of food?"

Mama said, "The Lord will provide a way."

All of us were cold and tired, but no one complained. As we gathered our things, Dilly begged,
"Somebody carry me." Then we started our all-
night march. I still felt guilty about almost losin' the
baby, so I picked her up and carried her long after
my arms ached like they were broken.

An owl was hootin', and you could see his big eyes
glowin' up in a tree. Our eyes had gotten used to the
dark, but we'd never be able to see as good as that
owl. Pretty soon he must have spotted what he was
lookin' for, 'cause he swooped away without a sound.

In the moonlight, you could see the bright eyes of
little ground animals. The leaves would rustle, and
they'd dash off. Once we thought we heard a wolf
howl, but he didn't bother us and we sure didn't
bother him.

As day broke I was about to ask if somebody else
could please carry Dilly. Just then Daddy said,
"Let's stop soon. We've gone a long way since this
time yesterday. I think we've gone far enough that
we can let up for awhile."

Mama pointed to two trees way back in the forest. She said, "I think that's a good stoppin' place."

When we'd started yesterday, we were still in the tall pines. Then we'd walked out of the pines and through the oak forest all night. Now we were surrounded by hickory trees.

We got out the last of the ham and bread and had breakfast. Carrie picked up a hickory nut. Knowin' how good hickory nuts taste, she said, "Mama, is this what you meant when you said, 'The Lord will provide a way'?"

Mama smiled and answered, "Maybe we should take some with us. You and Luther go gather some." So we did. We were careful not to break branches or do anything that would make a sound or show we'd been there. Just as we'd finished pickin' up all the nuts we could carry, I came upon a place where somebody had had a fire—not long before. We looked all around. No one was in sight. We hurried to tell Daddy and Mama.

"Makes you wonder who it was," said Mama.

Daddy added, "Could have been the slave catcher, lookin' for us. If it was, he's moved on north, and we don't want to catch up with him."

Carrie said, "Or it could have been other escapin' slaves, and somebody may have come lookin' for them and will catch us, too."

"Could be Indians also," I commented. "Not all the Indians have been forced away from here."

"That's true. If it is Indians, they would probably help us," Daddy told us.

We talked about what to do. We wondered whether to go, or stay, or what. We finally decided to keep goin' with our eyes and ears open.

It had been gettin' colder and colder. Today was bitter cold. The wind was whippin' through the trees. It would have been even worse if we'd been out in an open field, but it was bad enough with our hands and feet numb as we stumbled along beneath the trees. I could not remember ever bein' so cold in my chest and between my shoulder blades.

Mama was cold and knew we were, too. She said, "Rub your hands together." Carrie and I did, and our hands made a kind of whistlin' noise. Mama said, "Shhh, rub them more quiet."

I found that rubbin' my hands against my clothes and wigglin' my fingers helped a little.

Next time we got close enough to our stream to take a look, it was frozen. Daddy said that was good. "Gettin' farther north and deeper into winter," he said. "It's been cold here for days."

"Wouldn't it be wonderful if this cold weather froze that river we might have to cross?" asked Mama. "But I doubt it," she added.

"What river, Mama?" asked Carrie.

"The Mississippi."

"How will we get across it if it's not frozen?" I asked.

"We'll figure something out," said Daddy.

Carrie and I looked at each other. Of course we would try to find a way. We felt silly for askin'.

Meantime we were all so tired we were stumblin' along. We'd been walkin' since daybreak the day before. Mama and Daddy passed a few words between them, and Mama told us, "Let's stop. We're so tired, we're not makin' any speed."

Daddy said, "I think that fire must've been made by slave catchers who are lookin' for us. We don't want to catch up with 'em."

We huddled around the nearest tree. Leanin' against each other gave us warmth and a feelin' of togetherness.

Daddy took the first watch. He stood with his back against the trunk. Standin' there in the cold, he broke out in a sweat like it was summertime. Mama had fallen asleep but Dilly wiggled in Mama's arms and woke her up. Mama reached in her pocket and gave Dilly a sugar tit to suck on. Mama was about to go back to sleep when she noticed that Daddy was sweatin'. She laid Dilly against me and stood up to see about Daddy. He tried to act like he was all right so Mama wouldn't be worried.

"Harvey Lee Lawson, you can't fool me. You're sick," Mama said. She took the blanket off her shoulders and wrapped it around Daddy. He just kind of slid down the tree trunk from standin' to sittin' to lyin' down.

Mama knelt down beside him. "You been goin' too hard." Reachin' into her little drawstring bag, she said, "I bet you been feelin' bad ever since we set out, just didn't want to say nothin'."

Daddy kinda half smiled. "You know me real well, don't you, Emma Spurlark Lawson?"

Mama nodded and put her hand on Daddy's forehead. "Harvey Lee, you're burnin' up with fever!" She knew just what to do. She took some healin' roots out of her bag. She gave one to Daddy, sayin', "Here, chew this." As she talked, she made a little pile of leaves on the ground. Then she picked up some freezin' cold leaves and covered Daddy's chest with 'em.

Carrie woke up and saw what Mama was doin'. "Why you puttin' leaves on Daddy?" she asked.

Mama explained: "So they'll draw the heat out of his body."

Daddy raised up on one elbow and grinned as he said, "You children come put your hands under me and I'll warm 'em up." We did, and he did. But we were all worried. Would Daddy get well?

CHAPTER

6

Daddy and all the rest of us were wonderin', What now? None of us knew how sick he was. If he could get well, how long would it take? Would he be able to travel? How much danger were we in right now? Rememberin' what Daddy had said earlier about leavin' him behind if he didn't make it back to Cap'n's plantation, I was afraid he might tell us to go ahead without him.

Mama checked the leaves on Daddy's chest. The heat from his body had made them as dry and crisp as they could be. Mama told Carrie and me, "Here, warm your feet," and we tucked our feet into the pile of warm leaves. She put fresh leaves on Daddy's chest and some on his forehead. Finally he went to sleep but jerked and groaned so we got even more worried.

Daddy woke up as it was gettin' dark. He stretched and said, "I sure feel better, let's go. I'm ready if you are. I think we let those slave catchers put enough distance between us and them." We were all *so* happy Daddy was better. He really seemed all right. It was just like he hadn't been sick.

Before leavin' we made sure we left things lookin' like nobody had been there. We knew if bloodhounds came sniffin' around, they would get our scent. Then Carrie and I had an idea. We both picked up an armful of the leaves that had been on Daddy's chest and walked a good ways in different directions from the hickory tree. We even dropped hickory nut shells along our path. After that we went over to some pine trees that had grown among the hickories. We put our hands and arms all around the pine tree trunks as if we'd been climbin' them. Last thing we did was to walk backwards—back to the tree where our family was. That way, if the hounds led the slave catchers to our tree, they'd branch off in different directions, not knowin' which way we'd really gone. Carrie even tore off a little piece of her skirt and hung it on a thornbush so they'd think she had snagged her dress when she ran away.

Now we were all set to leave. We walked in pairs

toward the stream. It was frozen so solid we could walk on the surface. That was fun.

It was a pretty cloudy night. Mama said it looked like it might snow. And sure enough, a few big flakes began to fall. It didn't take long till the snow got heavy. That gave us a new problem to solve. We had to figure out some way not to leave four sets of tracks. We decided that we should walk in a line one behind the other. Mama went first. She was carryin' Dilly, so together they only made one set of footprints. Carrie followed in Mama's tracks, and I stepped in Carrie's. Daddy then stepped in mine so it would look like just one person had walked there.

The stream widened into a river. It was frozen over so we kept walkin' in each other's footsteps. We walked like this till it was almost day. Daddy said, "We got to stop soon. You-all have missed a lot of sleep. If you don't get some rest, you'll be sick, too."

Snow was still fallin' but it had started to cover up our tracks. It was a wet snow—the kind that sticks to your face, then rolls down your neck when it melts.

Carrie said, "You're tired, too, Daddy. I sure wish there was a way we could get out of this snow and get some rest. It'd be nice if we could all get some sleep without havin' to worry about somebody sneakin' up on us."

I'd been thinkin' the same thing. My rope might

be just the thing to solve our problem. "If we could find a good stoppin' place," I said, "I could tie my rope from tree to tree so it would fence off the place where we'd be sleepin'."

"That's good, Luther. The rope would trip any horse headin' our way. That would give us a warnin'," said Carrie.

"That would be kind of cruel to a horse, but it's our only chance to get some rest. Let's just hope no horses come along," said Daddy.

We had gotten into some rocky country. We found a spot protected by a big stone on one side and trees on the other. I tied my rope in place. The wind had blown snow over my tracks before I got back to the family. We sure were in luck.

We must have slept, huddled under our blanket, for hours, 'cause when we woke up it was the middle of the day. It was cloudy, though. The snow was still blowin'. It had changed from wet snow to the kind that stings your face.

"We better get movin'," said Mama.

I untied my rope. I sure felt proud I could use it so we could sleep safe and sound. Little had Cap'n or I known what a big help that rope would be. The day I'd asked, "Cap'n, can I have this old rope?" he'd said, "May as well take it, there's no more use in it." I thought to myself, Maybe not for trainin' horses . . .

We went back to the river. This time we walked along the bank, just in case the ice wasn't frozen solid as the river got wider. The river may not have been frozen, but our feet sure were. Still we had a lot to be thankful for.

Mama said, "It's good we have the river to follow or we wouldn't know which way was north."

The longer we walked, the worse the snowstorm got. The blowin' got so bad we could hardly see. Carrie said, "If we all hold onto Luther's rope, that will help us stay together."

Mama said, "Sounds like a good idea." So we held onto the rope. I used my free hand to hold Dilly's free hand. I wasn't goin' to take another chance with her. She didn't like me holdin' on to her, and every few minutes she let out a scream as she tried to make me let go of her hand. Lucky for us, we were the only people out in the snowstorm. We must have walked ten miles like that.

We were gettin' into hilly country, but of course the river always led us through lowlands and valleys. Just before nightfall we noticed an openin' on the side of a hill. From a distance, it looked like it might be big enough to crawl in. When we got to the openin', I stuck my head through. It wasn't just a hole. It was the entrance to a big open space inside the hill. We'd found another cave! We stepped inside out of the storm. It was much warmer there than outdoors, the perfect place to spend the night. We brushed the snow off our heads and shook it off our clothes. Carrie commented, "Do we dare make a fire with my flint stones?"

Suddenly we heard a deep bass male voice say, "Welcome to my cave."

CHAPTER

7

We didn't know whether to run or stay—or if we were already trapped. We looked around in the darkness, but couldn't see where the voice came from. Before we could do anything, the mystery voice spoke again. It echoed from the sides, top, and bottom of the walls. It said, "I've been watchin' and listenin' ever since you headed for my cave." We were still huddled together, tremblin' when "the voice" laughed like it'd really enjoyed playin' a joke on us. Then whoever was makin' the voice stopped laughin' and sounded like he really meant it. "Relax, I'm not goin' to hurt you. Make yourself at home."

We wanted to believe that the man really meant what he said. But we were still wonderin', Have we walked into a trap? Are there other people hidin' in this cave? Who are they? What are they up to? Why are they here?

"I guess that was a pretty mean trick. I'm here by myself all the time and thought it would be fun to keep you guessin'," the voice went on.

"Who are you?" called Daddy. His voice echoed, too.

The voice said, "I'm a fugitive just like you. I escaped from a plantation near Palmyra, but my wife is in Hannibal. I stay here so that once in a while I can slip over to her place and see her."

"We know how you must feel tryin' to stay in touch," Mama said.

The man continued: "I could have got away, since the Fabius River ran right by the plantation I was on. It leads to the Mississippi, you know."

"No, we don't know, tell us," said Daddy.

"The river outside this cave leads to the Fabius," the man continued. "The Mississippi is just about a half day from here. It's frozen over now. You might can scooch across on your stomachs like the Indians know to do."

"Why on our stomachs?" I asked.

"Ice is less likely to crack that way," the man answered.

"Emma, you did ask me if we might have to cross the Mississippi," said Daddy.

"And now we know there is a way to cross it," answered Mama. "We can go across on the ice!"

The man chuckled. "Folks around here call it the 'Jack Frost Bridge.' "

Carrie and I laughed, too. This was the first time any of us had been able to laugh—or speak—out loud in days.

The man told us: "Try to cross the river so you're at the Van Doren Sawmill when you reach the other side. 'Most every Sunday there's a black preacher who holds a skillet in a way that makes his voice carry across the river. He says folks at that sawmill help slaves."

Carrie repeated, "Van Doren. I wonder if I could read those words for us."

Mama patted her on the shoulder. "I 'magine you could."

"Don't worry," said the man, "it's the only sawmill you'll see."

"Oh, good." Carrie sounded kind of relieved.

"I think you're best off stayin' here till this time tomorrow night," said the man.

"Where are you?" Daddy asked. "I just want to shake your hand and say, 'Thank you!' Talkin' to you makes me feel like we can really make it to freedom."

The man came out from the shadows to shake hands with Daddy. He said, "Good luck, brother." He was handsome and young, but he had worry lines in his face. A slingshot was stuck in his back pocket.

"Won't you come with us?" asked Daddy.

"I can't leave my wife," explained the man. "She's afraid to escape. She's seen some horrible punishments given when fugitives get caught. So, I guess I'll spend the rest of my days here to be near her."

"I wish you well," said Daddy. "And thank you for what you told us. We'll rest a lot easier tonight."

"Before you came in here I was just about to cook supper. Won't you join me?" asked the man.

"Cook?" all of us asked at once.

"Yes, I make a fire in here, and the smoke goes out high in the hills. Ain't no slave catchers found it yet, and I been here two years. How about some roasted rabbit? I went huntin' with my trusty slingshot today." The thought of hot, roasted food sounded so good our stomachs growled before we could say anything.

We gathered around as the man made the fire. He seemed glad to have company and said, "When dinner's finished, I'll show you to your rooms." Sure enough, after the best dinner in the world, he lit a pine knot and used it like a torch to show us around his "castle."

First he led us to a room where the rocks hung down like giant icicles. He told Mama and Daddy, "Here, you take the Crystal Room." Then he showed us a room with a high ceilin', like a big beautiful church. Carrie said, "This looks like a cathedral I saw in a book once. I'd like to stay here with Dilly," so she did. Nearby, he took me up some rocks that were just like stair steps. They led to an upstairs "room." "You might like this room because there's a place where you can look out," he said, pointin' to an openin' in the "roof." "You can see the sky from here, and best of all, if you climb out through this openin', you can see what's happenin' on the ground for miles around. I spend most of my time up here. I don't want any slave catcher to ever take me by surprise."

I stuck my head out the top. The view was wonderful. "Oh, thank you!" I cried.

"You're welcome," said the man. "We have to help each other. Well, I'm goin' to go see my wife now."

"Good luck!" I cried.

He thanked me and said, "I'll need it. It's dangerous out there." Sayin' that must have reminded him to add, "If you-all leave here about this time tomorrow night, you should be able to get to the river and cross over to Quincy by the next mornin'."

"What state is Quincy in?" I asked.

"Illinois," he told me.

"Do they have slaves there?"

"No. Illinois is a Free State. But slave catchers

can go over there and snatch you. That's what worries my wife."

"Where can we go to be safe?" I asked.

"I've heard you're not safe till you get to Canada," said the man. He looked up at the night sky as if he could tell time by the stars. "Well, got to go now, good night."

Our host started down the steps, then turned and said, "By the way, my name is Marcus, Marcus Jackson. I didn't say my name before, 'cause I was afraid if you got caught, they'd force you to tell them about my wife and me. But I know now that I can trust you-all."

After he left, I climbed through the openin' in the roof again. Pine scrubs grew all around the hole, keepin' the snow from blowin' in. The snow had stopped, and the moon was bright, but the wind was strong enough to blow the snow into drifts. I could see Marcus makin' his way toward his wife's place in Hannibal. The driftin' snow covered his tracks each time he made a step. I was asleep when he came back.

The next day was the freest and happiest our family had ever had. Outside, it was snowin' again. But we were inside—all together—without anyone givin' us orders. We played house in a warm, roomy cave, laughin' and talkin' like never before.

It was the first time we'd had a chance to have a long talk with Daddy since before he was sold. He told us about things that had happened after he was a coachman in Waverly.

He said, "I drove the massa a lot of places. While he was takin' care of his business, I'd be out in the stable talkin' and listenin'. There'd be coachmen, jockeys, trainers—all kinds of folk who work with horses. I even met stagecoach drivers and Pony Express riders."

"I wish I could have been there and heard all that horse talk," I said.

"We talked 'bout more'n horses," explained Daddy. "A lot of those folk had done far travelin' with their massas. Why, one jockey had even been way up in Canada to race horses."

Mama said, *"Canada?* Did he say what part of Canada?"

"Yes," Daddy answered. "He said he was in a place called London."

Carrie yelled, "London. I saw a book, back when Cap'n's daughter, Susan, was teachin' me to read. It said London is a big city in England. Do you 'spose Canada has a city called London, too?"

Daddy said, "Maybe so. Anyway, that's what the jockey said. And I've been thinkin' that that might be a place to go look for a job."

Mama smiled. "I'll be happy when we get away from slavery and go someplace where we get *paid* for workin'."

We could tell that Marcus enjoyed havin' company for a change, the way he made us feel so welcome. He seemed to feel guilty about relaxin' with us, though. He said that he usually kept a close watch on what was goin' on outside his cave. And that visitin' with us, he'd let down his guard.

After enjoyin' the day, we had a delicious stew Marcus made from wild onions and other root plants he had gathered in the fall and stored in a cool cave room. He cooked the vegetables in the gravy he had saved from the roast rabbit.

After dinner Marcus said, "Guess you-all best get ready. If you leave soon after dark, you should get to the Mississippi River and 'cross by mornin'. Sure wish my wife and I could join you."

We thanked him and went to gather our things. I went up to "my room" to be sure I had everything. Daddy and Marcus were sayin' their good-byes near the bottom of "my stairs." Carrie was in "my room" lookin' at the view from the roof. "Daddy, Marcus," she called suddenly, "somebody is comin' to the cave!" I climbed up next to Carrie and saw someone walkin' up the hill in the blowin' snow.

"I'll go down to greet 'em," said Marcus. He took his slingshot out of his pocket and went toward the entrance of the cave.

Daddy told me, "Let me come take a look from where you are."

As the stranger got closer, we saw it was a woman

holdin' her long skirts up as she ran. "Who do you suppose she is?" I asked.

Carrie cried, "It must be Marcus's wife!"

We all looked at each other in horror and bolted down to where Marcus was.

He was standin' just inside the cave entrance. He had his deadly slingshot ready so that the minute the stranger entered the cave, he could let 'em have it. He tightened his grip and pulled back on the strap.

The woman appeared in the doorway callin' "Marcus!" at the same minute we were tryin' to warn him.

He had enough time only to change his aim a bit. A rock whizzed past his wife's arm and smashed against the wall.

"Marcus! It's me, Dicey!"

Marcus staggered forward and nearly passed out in his wife's arms. "Oh, Dicey, darlin', I almost killed you!" His deep voice was hoarse and tremblin'.

Dicey hugged him real tight and talked fast. "But you didn't kill me, and I'm all right. I was so upset, I forget to use the signal we'd planned. I forgot about everything except gettin' here, tellin' you I'm goin' to be sold tomorrow! We got to run away, now!"

Marcus finally pulled himself back. He looked kind of happy when he told Dicey, "I've been

waitin' a long time to hear you say that. Let's go."
As soon as he gathered up his belongin's, we
started out. He led the way along the little river
until we reached the Fabius River. Then we
walked until we came to the Mississippi.

Marcus said, "Well, this is it." He explained to
Dicey how we were goin' to slide across on our
bellies.

We were in kind of a level, wooded spot where we
could lay facedown on the riverbank, then slide onto
the ice. Marcus went first. When he got out about
six feet, Dicey followed. She tried to be ladylike,
and instead of layin' flat on the riverbank and easin'
herself onto the ice, she knelt down on the hard
surface. The ice cracked! Dicey was able to scram-
ble back on shore but Marcus was stranded!

CHAPTER

8

If Marcus tried to slide straight back to shore, the ice would give way. If he tried to slide around the place where the ice broke, he might open up a crack.

I clutched my rope, feelin' helpless as I watched Marcus struggle for his life. Then I thought, My rope might give him something to hang on to. Quickly, I blurted out my idea, and Dicey, Mama, Daddy, and Carrie tied one end of the rope to a tree, then took hold like you do when you're playin' tug-of-war. I threw the free end of the rope out to Marcus. He caught it and tried to swing around the spot where the ice was cracked. But about three feet from the shore, the ice gave way again and Marcus started to sink.

We pulled for all we were worth. With all of us workin' together, Marcus was able to get back to the riverbank. Dicey stretched out her arms to him, then burst into tears. "Marcus, you waited all these years for me, and then I almost caused you to drown. Oh, Marcus, forgive me!"

Marcus put his arm around her shoulders and said, "You forgave the awful thing I did earlier. We're all right now. That's the important thing." He looked at the rest of us and said, "Hey, let's get goin'. We don't have time for me to relax. We've got a river to cross before daylight!"

He got up and led the way up the riverbank. Again he lay down on his belly and slid onto the ice. Dicey did the same thing.

We followed one by one. Carrie and I each held one of Dilly's hands to guide her as we scooched across the frozen river. Dilly giggled the whole time, but her laughter wasn't loud enough to be heard for any distance.

There were about six ships stranded in the middle of the river. Marcus said when boats got frozen in like that, their crews painted them and got them ready for the spring thaw. I know one thing, we were glad to be hidden by their shadows. It seemed like the river was at least a mile wide, and in the moonlight, someone on shore could have seen the seven of us wigglin' our way across the ice.

The sun was just comin' up when we got to the Illinois side of the river.

As it turned out, we came off the ice just below the sawmill Marcus had told us about. At first we didn't know how close we were to the mill, but as we hid in the bushes along the shore, Marcus went to check. In just a moment, he came back and said, "We came out exactly where we want to be. If we'd crossed where we first started to, we would have been too far downstream." Then he told us, "You wait here till I see if it's safe for us to go up to the mill." Marcus was barely out of sight when we heard horses approachin' along the riverbank. Dilly had been half asleep. She perked up when she heard the animals and screamed, "Horsey! Horsey! I want to see horsey!"

Mama whispered, "Shh" and clamped her hand firmly over Dilly's mouth.

"It's the boogeyman. Be quiet so he won't get you," ordered Carrie.

Dilly's eyes opened wide in fright. Mama stuck a sugar tit in her mouth. "Dilly," she said, "your face feels awfully warm." She touched Dilly's forehead. "I hope you're not comin' down with what Daddy had." But there was no time to talk.

The horses were very close by, now. "Crouch down and don't make a sound," Daddy told us. He crawled to the edge of the bushes. I realized he was plannin' to distract the horsemen if they came any nearer. The horses stopped not fifty feet from us. We heard one horseman's voice sayin', "I think we've come far enough." Then the horses whirled around and headed toward the sawmill.

Daddy crawled back. "Have mercy!" he said. "Thank the Lord those slave catchers left us alone."

"But what about my Marcus, they ridin' the way he went," said Dicey.

Daddy put his hand on her shoulder. "I'm sure Marcus will be all right. He knows what to do. We should take turns restin' while we're waitin' for him. This might be our only chance to rest up. No tellin' what the rest of the day will be like."

Dicey insisted on takin' the first watch. After what seemed like hours we heard a rustlin' in the bushes. "Shh," said Daddy. Mama looked at Dilly who was still suckin' on her sugar pacifier. Just before my heart pounded right out of my chest, Marcus stuck his head through the bushes and signaled us to follow him. One by one we did.

As we got closer, Carrie could hardly walk, she was so excited about readin' the name on the mill. "Van Doren." She stumbled and almost fell. Pullin' on my sleeve she said, "Luther, Luther, I can read it!"

"Hurry up, Carrie, you're slowin' us down," I said. But I was really wishin' I knew how to read, too.

At the sawmill, I couldn't believe my ears when we were greeted by a white man who was about the age of Cap'n, but who said the opposite of what Cap'n would have said. "Welcome, I'm glad you got away." He walked over to some wagons. "You're going to have to hide," he told us, "to avoid the slave hunters who come across the border to recapture slaves." Marcus turned to Dicey when he heard the words "slave hunters." He told her, "I just had a close call with three slave catchers while walkin' back to where you all were waitin' for me. Lucky I heard them in time to hide. They came within ten feet of where I was crouched."

Dicey clutched his hand and whispered, "Oh, Marcus, you don't know how scared I was that those three men had got you!" Marcus smiled and bent over, kissin' her on the head.

The man, who never did tell us his name, said, "We don't have any time to lose. Those slave catchers will be back." He walked over to some wagons. "You're going to have to hide down in the bottom of these lumber wagons, so we can take you to the Underground Railroad stations."

"Underground Railroad stations?" I asked. "What're those?"

"They're secret hiding places provided by people who want to bring an end to slavery. You'll hide here in Quincy until night, then you'll start on your trip north."

So we climbed into the wagons: Dicey and Marcus in one, Carrie and me in another, and Mama and Daddy and Dilly in a third. I noticed that the horses hitched to Mama and Daddy's wagon had little bells on their harnesses.

The lumberyard workers began to pile planks over us in such a way that the first planks formed a false bottom in the wagon. They loaded the wagon with lumber, but they left space above us. I knew because I could look through the cracks and see blue sky.

To our surprise, we heard the lumbermen talkin' about takin' each wagon to a different place. How awful! We were about to be separated from our parents, Dilly, and Marcus and Dicey. With all we'd gone through to try to escape and stay together, how could they do this horrible thing to us?

We listened to the voice of the man about Cap'n's age. He said, "I sure hate to separate a family, but there's so much heat on now. The Adams County sheriff is taking fugitive slaves back to Missouri almost as fast as they can cross the river. A party of seven fugitives couldn't get to the edge of town without being captured. I think this family is safest this way."

Daddy and Mama must have thought they could trust the man, 'cause they didn't put up a fuss. Instead, Daddy called to us from his wagon. "God bless you, children. We'll try to get to London. We'll look for you there." Mama was cryin' as she said,

"We love you." I was numb with anger and fright. Dilly called, "Bye-bye." Carrie sobbed and cried out to Mama and Daddy.

The horses on our wagon whinnied.

A lumberman's voice said, "Where must we take 'em, boss?"

I guess the man who'd met us was the boss, 'cause he said, "Take the older couple to the Everett House in town. That's closest to the Chicago, Burlington and Quincy Railroad. I understand that Dr. Dyer has some railway coaches set aside for fugitives on the train that leaves about nightfall."

Another wagon driver asked, "Will we ever take passengers to Doc Eel's house again?" The boss answered, "Oh, no. After the court case and Dr. Eel's death, that station went out of business for good."

"Stephen A. Douglas was the judge in that case, wasn't he?" someone asked.

"Yes . . . ," the boss answered. He sounded as if he was goin' to add something else when I heard our driver ask, "Where should we go then, boss?"

"Take the young couple to the Number One Station at Mission Institute, and the children to Professor Nelson's house. Be on your way now."

With that, the wagons rolled out of the lumberyard. For awhile, we could hear the wheels of three wagons and the sound of the horses cloppin' along on the cobblestones. I could tell which one was

Mama and Daddy's wagon by the sound of the little bells. We could hear the early-mornin' noises of the city—of people greetin' each other as they came to market.

Pretty soon, we heard one wagon turn down a different street. It was the wagon Mama and Daddy and Dilly were in. I couldn't hold my tears back any longer. It was awful to feel we might never see them again. And worse, for none of us to be able to do anything about it—or to even hug each other good-bye.

Although our family had been split up when Daddy was sold, we'd always hoped we could get back together or at least Daddy could come over to New Franklin every once in a while. Now, Carrie and I might have lost our parents and Dilly forever! We were both cryin' as our wagon rode on.

Dicey and Marcus's wagon was still beside ours, but that wasn't much comfort. We knew they would soon go someplace other than where we were goin'.

We rode and rode till finally one wagon driver yelled to the other, "We're at the Mission Institute. Wonder if Professor Nelson is here." The second driver yelled back, "He might still be at home." The first driver answered, "Let's check and see." Both wagons came to a stop. Durin' our ride we'd found a little knothole in the side and had taken turns lookin' out. We could see about twenty little buildings sittin' in a meadow. That must be what they called the Mission Institute.

Our driver took the wagon down a long road. A man was walkin' across the meadow toward us. Our driver stopped, and the man said, "Good morning, what brings you here today?"

"We have two 'packages.' I have a boy and girl in my wagon. There's a man and woman in the other wagon," answered the driver.

"Leave the adults here at the institute," said the man. "The students can get them over to the Illinois River route."

The wagon Marcus and Dicey were in pulled away from ours. Carrie whispered to me, "There go the last two people we know." I knew they couldn't hear me but I whispered, "Good-bye, Marcus, good-bye, Dicey."

"Thanks for everything—especially the roasted rabbit," Carrie added.

Our driver asked the man, "What must I do with the children, Professor Nelson?"

"Take them to my house," he said. "I'll get my horse and meet you there." Our wagon continued down the road. Finally we reached what must have been Professor Nelson's house. It was surrounded by trees. Our driver stopped. He removed the planks from over us.

Carrie and I jumped down from the wagon. The driver said, "Good luck to you. I've got to deliver this load of lumber now," and he headed back to town.

Carrie and I stood in the road wonderin' what was goin' to happen next.

Professor Nelson rode up beside us. He got off his horse and introduced himself. He was kind of plain lookin'. He invited us into the house and said, "I understand what it's like to be hunted down. I was chased from Missouri over to Quincy by a pro-slavery mob."

He introduced us to his children, but not to his wife. Then he showed us to a trapdoor on the second floor. It led to a little brick room behind the fireplace. We felt warm and safe there, although mostly we were feelin' sad about being separated from Mama and Daddy. Two of Professor Nelson's children brought us some breakfast and a few clothes. He had quite a few children, and I don't remember their names. The children told us their father had owned slaves until he realized how wrong it was. But their mother didn't share all their father's views. That explained why she hadn't made an effort to meet us. Anyway, we spent the day in that little brick room.

Just after dark—about the time that Mama and Daddy must have been gettin' on the railroad train— several of the Nelson children came to our waitin' place and took us down to the basement. On the way they said their father was an Underground Railroad "agent." They talked about how he and other agents would help us on our way toward Canada.

Professor Nelson was waitin' at the foot of the steps to show us a tunnel that went from the basement to a clump of bushes out in the yard. He pointed the way to a place called Mendon, the next stop on the Underground Railroad. It was a little more than ten miles northeast, he said. As he pointed, I looked up at the night sky and thought, That means we go toward the North Star, but bear to the right. He told us to be on the lookout for a big red barn.

Carrie and I were on our own. "Luther, we don't have anybody but ourselves," she said. "That's kind of scary when you think about it."

"Sure is, but we'll be all right." I didn't want to think about it anymore, so I said, "Let's go find that red barn."

"We can take turns leadin' the way," said Carrie. "I'll go first."

We walked all night through dense forests and frozen fields. Two or three times we thought we heard someone comin'. We stopped and hid. It must have been our imagination, 'cause we never saw anybody. At first light of day, it was Carrie's turn to lead the way. She spotted the big red barn way off in the distance. We were so happy we felt like runnin' to it, but we knew that could be dangerous, so we took our time and tried not to be seen.

When we got to the barn, we didn't see anyone stirrin' around there or at the nearby farmhouse. We decided to go in and wait to see what would happen. We hid in the hayloft. It was good to be indoors. The barn wasn't very warm, but it was much better than bein' outdoors.

Carrie seemed to be catchin' a cold. She hadn't told me but I'd heard her sneeze once or twice while we were walkin'.

Pretty soon an elderly farmer came to the barn. Without lookin' up, he said, "Good morning" with an accent. Then he sat down on a stool to milk his cow. When he was through, he stood under the hayloft and said, "How 'bout some fresh milk for breakfast?"

We leaned out and thanked him.

He asked, "Are your parents with you?"

We looked at each other wonderin' how he knew we'd been travelin' with our parents. Then we told him, "No, they went on a train instead."

"Oh," he said, pullin' out a newspaper notice.

Carrie reached down and asked, "May I see that?" The man looked surprised, but pleased, to see that she could read. She read the paper out loud. "It says here: 'A family of five escaped,' and then it tells something about each of us. And look, it even mentions the lash marks on my back, but they call 'em scars instead of lash marks!"

"My goodness," I said, "maybe splittin' up *has* kept us from bein' caught. The slave hunters might go right on past us two."

"I sure hope so!" said Carrie.

We had expected to stay in Mendon that day, but later on the farmer rushed into the barn and yelled, "Come. I must take you on to the next town. Two of Professor Nelson's children just came to warn us that Mose Twist, the notorious slave kidnapper, is looking for your family in Quincy. He may soon head this way." He got his wagon ready and had us help him load it with big barrels of tallow. (I don't know why, but he called them "hogsheads" of tallow.)

The farmer seemed as worried as we were about the danger we were in. I asked him what made him decide to help us. He said, "I was a boy in Europe, and my parents were persecuted. I came to America to be free."

The last two barrels were fakes. They had tallow at the top and were hollow underneath.

After we loaded everything onto the wagon, the farmer told Carrie and me to climb up and hide inside the hollow barrels. Carrie squeezed into one, and I squeezed into the other. I felt closed in, but I had to admit it was warmer in there than in the open wagon. I was glad because my fingers were freezin'. Holes let in enough air so I could breathe. I could hear the farmer's voice. He said, "We're bound for Plymouth town."

We hadn't gone far when the farmer said, "We got away just in time. I see Mose Twist and his boys ridin' up to my barn. They might follow us." Sure enough, they did.

Pretty soon, I could hear horses gallopin' up on either side of the wagon. I was even more scared than I'd been that mornin' when we were spyin' on the three slave catchers. Then I heard a horse's whinny and what must have been Mose Twist's voice yellin', "Say, farmer, what you got in these barrels?"

"I've tallow, sir," answered the farmer.

"Well, do you mind if we open a few barrels? We're looking for some runaways," said Mose Twist.

"I'd rather you wouldn't, but if you insist, you may."

Luckily the barrels we were hidin' in were kind of in the center of the wagon, so they couldn't be reached by a man on horseback. But we had no way of knowin' whether Mose Twist and his men would stay on their horses. After all they were in the business of findin' folks.

I held my breath. My heart was poundin' like a drum. I knew Carrie was just as scared. I sure hoped she wouldn't sneeze.

9

The kidnappers didn't find us. "Five slaves couldn't just disappear, maybe they went the river route," said Mose Twist. He and his men wheeled their horses around and galloped away. I said a little prayer they wouldn't find Dicey and Marcus.

Our next stop was with the Adkins family in Plymouth. They made their own soap and candles from the farmer's tallow, and they supplied soap and candles to folks for miles around. They were anxious to hear how we'd escaped and found our way through Missouri with our parents, and about crossin' the Mississippi River, then bein' on our own. After dinner, we stretched out on pallets on the upstairs floor.

This was our first chance to talk to one another and stretch since being in those barrels. "I sure am glad we got here—safe," said Carrie.

"Me, too," I agreed.

"I thought Mose Twist was goin' to open our barrel. What if he'd found one of us, and not the other?" she said.

"Oh, I don't even want to think about it. What do you think is goin' to happen next?"

"I don't know, but I'm goin' to try to get some sleep."

I was sleepy, too. I kind of dozed on and off. When I woke up one time I heard a lot of talkin' downstairs. It sounded like a meetin' goin' on. The talk got louder and louder.

All evenin' there were people callin' each other "Deacon." There was talk of the Presbyterian and Congregational churches. "I think the church should speak out and act against slavery," said one person. Another answered, "Just give it time. The church is sure to come around." Somebody else said, "But we don't have time! I say slavery has got to be abolished now!"

Carrie woke up. She reached over from her pallet and hit me with her elbow. "Hey, Luther, do you hear what I hear?"

"Yeah, I'm gettin' an earful." I tried to stay awake and listen some more, but I fell sound asleep.

When I woke up, the meetin' had ended, and I didn't hear any sounds downstairs. It was still pitch dark outside. I turned over and went to sleep.

The next thing I knew, Mrs. Adkins was shakin' me. "Wake up. Wake up. You must leave now. You've got to get to the stagecoach road by early mornin'." She started downstairs as Carrie and I got our belongin's. "Bring your blankets," she added.

Downstairs she handed us some lunch and stepped outside. The family's big friendly dog ran along beside us as we followed her about a mile to a frozen river. It was much narrower than the Mississippi; in fact, a fallen tree served as a bridge from one side to the other.

"This is the LaMoine River," said Mrs. Adkins. "Follow it until you get to a road. There's a log cabin right where the river meets the road. If there's a lantern in the window, knock three times and a man will open the door. If there is no lantern, hide under the bridge until you see the man come out of the cabin." Then she chuckled. "That man's a squatter there, and for some strange reason, he likes to be called 'Deacon.' "

Just for the fun of it we decided to pretend we were skatin'. We figured if the mighty Mississippi was frozen solid enough to hold our weight, the ice on this narrower river would certainly be thick enough for skatin'. We were havin' such a good time glidin' along the ice, it seemed like we got to the bridge in no time.

But there was no light in the cabin window. Carrie said, "Do you 'spose somethin' is wrong?" The sky was so dark we would have seen even the least little light inside. We huddled under the bridge, wonderin': Are Mose Twist and his kidnappers nearby? Did anybody see us? Had we giggled or made some noise without realizin' it?

We heard a sound in the cabin. We crouched down, stiff with fear, and saw a grown man come out who didn't weigh as much as me. In the moonlight we could see that he had long, blondish hair and a beard. He struggled to carry a big trunk over to the side of the road. Then he came down to the riverbank toward us. "Mornin'," he said.

Frightened, we answered, "Good mornin'."

"Come on in the cabin and have some coffee. We have to get ready to catch the stage."

We wondered why he didn't seem to be in a hurry. And why he didn't have his lantern on when we got there.

As if he knew what we were thinkin', he said, "I usually keep the lantern on, but when the stage came through yesterday, the driver told me that slave catchers have even been hangin' round Galesburg! That made me kind of nervous, 'cause that's usually the safest place in these parts. So I decided to turn out the lantern and hope for the best."

He led the way to the road. "Now, here, climb in this trunk. It has air holes so you can breathe. Do you want to put your blankets in to pad the inside?"

Carrie and I nodded. We climbed into the big old trunk. Pretty soon we could hear horses and a carriage comin' toward us on the bumpy road. I got the same closed-in feelin' as when we had to hide in the fake tallow barrels. "I don't like bein' stuffed in tight places," I told Carrie.

"Me neither, but at least we both fit in here."

Deacon flagged down the stagecoach.

The driver said, "Good morning, Deacon. You going to Galesburg?"

"Yep. Got some business to take care of."

The driver loaded the trunk on top of the stagecoach with Carrie and me inside, and away we went. For a long time we could hear only the sounds of the wheels, the horse hooves, and once in a while, a cow mooing. Then we began to hear the sounds of people comin' and goin'.

In Galesburg, we stayed in the home of a black woman, Susan Richardson. Not only had she been a slave, but one of her children had been killed in a work accident and two other children had been taken away by a cruel owner. Now she lived in a little house all alone and earned her livin' by doin' laundry.

She treated us like we were her very own children. First, she said, "Please call me Mother Richardson." Then she asked, "What's your favorite food?"

Together, Carrie and I answered, "Sweet potato puddin'!"

"I've got some sweets down in the root cellar," she exclaimed. "Let me see what I can stir up."

After a delicious supper, she said, "Now you children get some rest while I stand watch. A day or so ago there were some slave stealers hangin' around the city. We think they're gone, but I'm goin' to be on the lookout, just in case."

The next mornin' we woke up to the smell of hot biscuits. We could have stayed with that nice woman forever, and she asked if we wanted to. She told us that Galesburg was a good town. "A lot of people at Knox College worked against slavery. Both black and white children can go to school here." She was quiet for a minute, then continued: "You could stay at my house and go to school. You could be my family."

That sounded like a wonderful idea, but neither Carrie nor I answered right away. I knew both of us were thinkin' the same thoughts. We could go to school and learn to read and write real well. We could maybe even go to college in Galesburg. We'd be in a town where we could feel pretty safe and not have to run and hide from slave catchers all the time. And we'd have a family again—and so would Mother Richardson.

Carrie spoke first. "Mother Richardson, thank you so much. We would just *love* to stay with you and go to school, but . . ."

I finished the sentence, ". . . we *have* to try and find our parents in Canada. So we got to keep goin'—as much as we would like to stay on here."

Mother Richardson understood but looked sad for awhile. She must have been thinkin' about her own children. All of a sudden she stood up and went into her wash shed to get each of us a coat and some boots. "Bundle up, children. You got a long ways to go." Then, changin' the subject, she asked, "Did you know it snowed last night?"

Oh, no, I thought, rememberin' how we trudged through snow when we were with our parents.

"I worked out a plan for you to get a sleigh ride to Princeton," Mother Richardson told us.

We got our things together, and soon there was a knock at the door. It was Brother Charles Gilbert. We hugged Mother Richardson good-bye and climbed into the sleigh. Jokingly she said, "Hide under that seat like you're two bundles of fresh laundry, now."

Carrie and I kissed Mother Richardson before we crawled under the seat.

Sleigh bells jingled as we rode along. Once we got way out of town, Brother Gilbert told Carrie and me, "I think you will be safe if you sit up on the seat." We climbed up. We could see for miles. The runners on the sleigh left lines in the snow. There were no other sleigh trails or signs of activity.

Ridin' along, I started thinkin' about Brother Gilbert and Mother Richardson, and how other black and white people had worked together and risked a lot for us. Back on the plantation, we hadn't had any idea that there were people like this. It was good to learn that they existed.

We ate supper and stayed overnight in a town named Osceola after a great Seminole chief. The next morning Brother Gilbert hitched up his horses, and we headed for Princeton.

We passed farms and little towns until finally, just before nightfall, we pulled into the yard of a big two-story farmhouse. Brother Gilbert explained: "This is Reverend Owen Lovejoy's house. His brother Elijah used to print an antislavery paper down in Alton, Illinois. But the press was pushed into the river, and Elijah was killed."

We went into the kitchen and warmed ourselves by the fireplace. There seemed to be a meetin' goin' on in a room toward the back of the first floor. We couldn't see into the room but we could hear things like:

"That Abe Lincoln will be an interesting fellow to watch."

"I sure wish we could get him to join the new Republican party."

"He's always been a good lawyer, but I was most

impressed when he gave that Peoria speech, where he said, 'When the white man governs himself, that is self-government; but when he governs himself and also governs another man, that is more than self-government, that is despotism.' "

"Lincoln's got a lot of ability. He'd make a good president!"

"Oh, come now, gentlemen, that's wishful thinking."

After eatin' a bowl of warm soup, Carrie and I followed Mrs. Lovejoy. We tiptoed up the stairs and into a room on the second floor. Mrs. Lovejoy took some heavy quilts off a shelf.

"I can't wait to get under those quilts," I told Carrie. "I still feel chilled—even after standin' by the fireplace and eatin' soup."

"I feel like my cold is gettin' worse," she said. She sounded miserable.

Mrs. Lovejoy gave us two quilts apiece. "You'll feel better after a good night's sleep," she told us.

We fell asleep immediately but were awakened later by a loud knock on the front door. Someone shouted, "Open up in the name of the law! Reverend Lovejoy, I have a warrant for the arrest of five escaped slaves—and you, too, if you're harboring them."

"Oh, Sheriff, I don't have any five slaves," Reverend Lovejoy answered. Just then Mrs. Lovejoy tiptoed into Carrie's and my room with a dimly lit lantern in her hand. She didn't say anything. To my surprise, she opened a secret door that led to a hidden closet. Mrs. Lovejoy used a hand signal to tell us to step inside with our quilts, then closed the secret door. From our hidin' place inside we could still hear noisy voices downstairs.

The sheriff told Reverend Lovejoy, "Let me check just to be sure."

"Well, all right, but you're wasting your time," Reverend Lovejoy said.

Carrie chuckled softly when she heard his answer, but she sounded serious when she whispered, "The sheriff is after us!"

I whispered back, "If he finds us, he'll try to make us tell where Mama and Daddy and Dilly went— and who helped us get this far."

The sheriff searched the first floor, then came up the stairs and into the very room we'd just left. Judgin' by his voice, he sounded like he was standin' right outside the wall on the other side of the closet where we were hidin'. I was tremblin' so much I was sure he'd hear my knees knockin' together. Carrie was fightin' back a sneeze, and our lives depended on whether or not she could hold it back. It was scary to know if you coughed, sneezed, or swallowed, your whole life would be ruined!

IO

The sheriff finally left the Lovejoys' house, but Carrie and I still felt uneasy. That had been too close for comfort. We knew that after they couldn't find five fugitives, they might realize our family had divided up into smaller groups. They might even figure out that Carrie and I would be travelin' together and that Mama and Daddy would keep Dilly with them.

While Carrie and I were wonderin' what to do next, I put my hand in my pocket and touched the mramnuo Daddy had given me. The horse statue gave me an idea. I told Carrie if we could get a horse, we could take ourselves to the next stoppin' place.

"Maybe Reverend Lovejoy would let us have one," she suggested. "Maybe. I know one thing, the sooner we can leave, the better I'll like it!"

"Me, too."

"Luther, if we wrapped one blanket around both our shoulders, we could fool anybody who was lookin' for the two of us 'cause we'd be like just one person on the horse."

"Since it's night it might work. Or we might scare somebody if they thought we were one person with two heads."

"This is no time to be jokin', Luther," Carrie scolded. "Let's go talk to Reverend Lovejoy."

"I like your plan," said Reverend Lovejoy later, "but my riding horse is the only one I can spare. He's a fine horse but he isn't used to going long distances."

"I think I can coax him to go farther," I said.

Carrie told Reverend Lovejoy how good I was with horses. She said, "If anybody can get that horse to go a long way, Luther can."

"You're certainly welcome to try," said Reverend Lovejoy.

So he let us have the horse and told us how to follow the Illinois River to the Hossack house in Ottawa. But he warned us, "Be on the lookout for highway robbers who've been in these parts."

We set out, ridin' all night.

There were times we had to travel along narrow ledges. They were very dangerous, and I had to use my skill to manage the horse. "Luther, if you didn't know how to ride so well, we could have fallen down on the rocks," said Carrie. "I wish I knew how to handle horses like you do." I felt pretty proud to hear my sister say that.

As we followed the river, we wondered if Marcus and Dicey had taken the same trails—or if they had been captured. We'd been lucky—to avoid highway robbers and slave catchers—and we hoped Marcus and Dicey had been lucky, too.

Before daylight, we spotted a house high up on the river bluff. It looked just like the Hossack house Reverend Lovejoy had described. It was fancier than Cap'n's. Poor Cap'n would have had a fit if he found out an abolitionist had a finer house than a slaveholder!

We found a path up the steep hill to the house, tied our horse to the hitchin' post, and tapped on the kitchen window. John Hossack and his wife were eatin'. They opened the door and greeted us, then fixed plates for Carrie and me. For the next several hours, we sat talkin' around the table.

First, the Hossacks asked about us—what our life in slavery was like, where we'd escaped from, what sort of things had happened, and if we thought we'd ever find our parents. Carrie told 'em how good I

was at handlin' horses. And I told 'em how good Carrie could read.

Then we asked the Hossacks about themselves. They told us they'd come from Scotland. They went to Canada for awhile, then moved to Ottawa, where they'd been for about six years. They believed slavery was wrong. Mr. Hossack said, "No one is truly free until everyone is free."

Mrs. Hossack nodded. "John really means that, too. The first time he was entrusted with underground passengers, his wagon was stoned by workers on the Illinois-Michigan canal. No one was hurt, but there have been some close calls, and I'm sure there will be more."

"Don't worry, dear," said Mr. Hossack. "When a body is doing what is right and just, there is nothing to fear. That's enough talk about me. Let's tell the children about the canal. Conditions have improved around there, and this time of year, the canal is the best route to Chicago."

Mrs. Hossack added, "Even though the Illinois and the Des Plaines rivers connect Ottawa with towns near Chicago, boats can't get through. All travel used to be overland between here and there. In the early days there was a portage trail."

"What's a portage trail?" I asked.

John Hossack explained: "It's an overland path from one body of water to another. For many years

Indians, and later other travelers, would go as far as they could on one river, then carry their canoes overland. They continued in their canoes when they got to the next body of water. That was before stagecoach travel got popular."

Mrs. Hossack continued: "Finally, in the 1840s, the Illinois-Michigan canal was built, and now, in warm weather, boats can take people and produce from here to Chicago. Horses and mules walk by the side of the canal on towpaths and pull them along, but the paths aren't used much in winter."

"Did you say 'towpath'?" asked Carrie. "I know what a path is, but what does the 'toe' part mean? Is it like a toe on your foot?"

Mrs. Hossack laughed. "I guess it does sound that way. The 'tow' in the word towpath is spelled t-o-w. It just means to drag something behind you with a rope or chain."

Quickly, John Hossack drew something on a piece of paper. "Here's a map. It'll show you how to get to John Jones's house at Fifth and Madison streets in Chicago." He handed us the map and went on talking. "Speaking of Chicago, do you know who Chicago's first permanent settler was?"

Together Carrie and I said, "No."

"It was a black man named Jean Baptist Point du Sable," said Mr. Hossack.

Carrie and I leaned forward to hear more.

"Du Sable had a thriving trading post before I was born. Seventy-five years ago, he traveled through this area and went on to establish his business at the very place where the great city of Chicago stands today."

"Du Sable chose a really strategic location." said Mrs. Hossack.

"France, Spain, and England all wanted it because it was the gateway to vital waterways and fur-rich lands," explained Mr. Hossack.

We could have listened to the Hossacks all day and all night, but Mrs. Hossack said, "You better get some sleep so you can start out for Chicago tonight."

"I think my cold will be gone by mornin' if I get a good night's sleep," remarked Carrie.

"Good," I said. "A couple of times I've been scared you'd sneeze when slave catchers were close enough to hear."

We slept the rest of the day until sunset. Then I woke up and lay in bed thinkin'. Although I gave our horse the best care I could, he did a lot of gallopin' to bring Carrie and me between Princeton and Ottawa. I could tell he was tired, and I hadn't been sure he was goin' to make it up that steep bluff from the riverbank to this house. After all, Reverend Lovejoy had warned us that a ridin' horse wasn't used to goin' long distances. We were sure thankful he'd gotten us here, but I couldn't push him any farther. So we left the horse with the Hossacks, who said they'd get him back to Reverend Lovejoy. Then we started our trip on foot, takin' blankets and food that the Hossacks gave us.

II

Carrie and I walked along the towpath beside the frozen canal. We were lucky that there was no snow on the ground. We were glad we didn't have to worry about leavin' tracks.

We kept our eyes and ears open to make sure that no slave catchers were layin' in wait for us. We didn't see or hear anybody during the night, so we decided it'd be safe for us to keep walkin', even after the sun came up.

Marseilles was the first town we came to after leaving Ottawa. It faced the canal, so we went around the outer edge of town to keep from bein' seen. We were able to make better time than we expected. We kept on goin'. We passed Seneca and reached Morris by nightfall. We slept in a deserted barn—where fresh teams of horses were kept durin' the warm months when they were needed to pull canal boats. We were in Channahon before sundown the next day. Two rivers meet there, and it was a beautiful sight to watch the sunset from the haystack we'd found to sleep in.

Next mornin' we started out again and trudged on. We passed through other towns. Carrie said their names sounded romantic. But to be honest, by that time, all I could think about was gettin' to Chicago. One thing I do remember is that one town had a big stone pit.

Four nights later, Carrie and I stumbled into Chicago in our raggedy clothes, tired and hungry. We couldn't believe our eyes. There were so many boats in the harbor and so many carriages and horses and wagons on the street. People were goin' in and out of houses that were built close together.

We took out the map Mr. Hossack had drawn. We had to get from Bridgeport, where the canal and towpath ended, to downtown Chicago. Carrie read the street signs. We walked many long city blocks. Everywhere we looked there were new and different sights and sounds. Some of the people we saw smiled. Others seemed too busy to even notice us. Finally we found the home of Mr. and Mrs. John Jones.

At first, we were afraid to knock because two carriages outside let us know that they already had company, but tired as we were, we didn't have any choice. This was the only stoppin' place we knew of. (Later we learned that many Chicago families opened their homes to fugitive slaves, and the members of Quinn Chapel African Methodist Episcopal church housed slaves.)

The Joneses welcomed us like we were special guests. They took us right into their front parlor. Two men were sittin' there. I'll never forget how they looked. One was a black man with a head of white hair and a beard to match. The other was a white man with bright red hair. He also had a beard. Mr. Jones introduced us to them. The black man was Frederick Douglass. The white man was a Scotsman named Alan Pinkerton.

They told us something about themselves. First we listened to Frederick Douglass. "I know what you have suffered. I was a slave in the state of Maryland," he said. "My wife-to-be helped me escape. Since then I've been working to end slavery by speaking and writing." Mr. Jones added, "Mr. Douglass has written books and traveled extensively. He even published a newspaper called the *North Star*."

Next, Alan Pinkerton told us his story. "I'm a detective and a cooper, the fancy name for a barrel maker. Quite by chance, I solved my first detective

case when I went looking for reeds to make barrels with." Then Mr. Jones explained that Mr. Pinkerton had rowed his boat to an island near his home, then solved a case that had stumped the sheriff.

Carrie and I felt real proud when these men stood up and shook our hands. They said they admired us for escapin' and survivin' all our hardships. No matter how tired you are, when folks rave over you like that, it makes you feel mighty good.

After Frederick Douglass and Alan Pinkerton sat back down, Mrs. Jones said, "I know you must be awfully tired. You must want to eat and get a good night's rest."

She was so right.

The next mornin', we had breakfast with the Joneses. "Mr. Pinkerton has invited you to come spend the winter in his hometown of Dundee," said Mrs. Jones. "It's about fifty miles from Chicago." Before Carrie or I could ask why, Mr. Jones explained, "That plan would be good for several reasons. For one thing, you'd be less likely to be caught if you were not right here in the city. And you have to wait somewhere, because the river you'll have to cross to get to Canada won't be passable until early spring."

"Excuse me for buttin' in," I said, "but do you mean we can't go lookin' for our parents and Dilly till springtime?"

"Yes. I'm sorry, but that's true," answered Mrs. Jones.

"That may be too late," said Carrie.

"I know you are disappointed, but you'd be in much more danger if you went to Detroit to wait for the spring thaw," said Mr. Jones.

"I sure wish that wasn't so," I said.

"I wish it wasn't, but it is. There is one more advantage to waiting out the winter in Dundee. You'll be able to do odd jobs and earn some money."

"Earn some money?" I asked. "You mean we will get paid for workin'?"

"That's sure different from slavery," said Carrie. Then she got a worried look. "Mr. Pinkerton makes barrels, but we don't know how to make 'em."

"Mr. Pinkerton will probably hire you to do jobs you already know how to do," said Mr. Jones. Then he told us that he had also gone to work at a young age. His mother was a free mulatto woman, and his father a German settler in North Carolina. To make sure her son would never be taken into slavery, Mr. Jones's mother had arranged for him to leave home and become a tailor's apprentice.

Mr. Jones's wife, Mrs. Mary Richardson Jones, was the daughter of a black blacksmith in Memphis. She, like Susan B. Anthony, tried to get the same rights as free men. She met Mr. Jones when he was hired out to a Memphis tailor. After they got married, they moved to Chicago, where they'd lived for ten years. Now they owned property and enjoyed entertainin' men and women who shared their interest in human rights.

After breakfast, the Joneses had two more callers: a Dr. C. V. Dyer and a Mr. Philo Carpenter. Again we were introduced all around. I remembered hearin' the name of Dr. Dyer back in Quincy. So I asked, "Dr. Dyer, do you run a railroad?"

He looked so surprised! "Why, yes. How did you know?"

"Well," I explained, "our whole family escaped together, but when we got to Quincy, a man at the sawmill said it would be best for us to split up. He sent Mama and Daddy and Dilly on your train."

"That's singular that we should meet," Dr. Dyer said. Then he looked down at the floor. "I'm sad to say, I have no way of knowing how to reunite family members. I'll be glad when we Underground Railroad workers find a way to do that!"

Mr. Carpenter had come to write some letters for Mr. Jones. Mr. Jones explained: "I never had the chance to go to school. But I am gradually learning. Meanwhile, I have to ask my friend, Philo Carpenter, to handle my correspondence. Whenever you get a chance to learn the three R's, learn all you can."

I didn't want to sound disrespectful, but I said,

"We passed up a chance in Galesburg, 'cause we wanted to get to Canada and find our parents."

Carrie added, "I hope we can find our family and all of us can go to school in Canada."

Mr. Carpenter looked up from his writin' and said, "I hope so. As you know, the three R's are reading, writing, and arithmetic. I'm just here for the first two R's, as Mr. Jones, being wealthy, has already mastered the subject of mathematics. And I might add, without my help." We all smiled at that.

When Mr. Carpenter had finished writing, we had tea on the Jones's beautiful tea set. Carrie and I stayed there one more day. Then Mr. Jones took us in his carriage to Alan Pinkerton's in Dundee to stay for the next three months.

Mr. and Mrs. Pinkerton greeted us warmly. Their family and workers lived over the cooper shop.

When Mr. Pinkerton took us down to the shop, he showed us how barrels could be made to hold all kinds of things, like tallow and molasses. He even showed us his secret of strappin' barrels with reeds. After that, he hitched up his horses and took us to the banks of the Fox River. We got out, and he rowed us to the little island where the barrel reeds grew—and where he had solved the case that had made him a famous detective.

When we got back to the cooper shop, Mr. Pinkerton said, "We need to find jobs for the two of you. What kinds of things do you like to do?"

"I like to work with horses," I said.

"We have lots of horses here," he commented. "Would you like to work in the stable?"

"I sure would," I answered.

"How about you, Carrie?"

"I like to read."

"You could be a big help in the office. And there are some books there that you could read when things aren't too busy."

Carrie smiled.

We started work the next day and were really happy to be doin' things that we liked and even better, gettin' paid for them.

By the time we paid Mrs. Pinkerton for our room and board, we didn't have much left over, but it was still wonderful to be earnin'.

One evenin' after work, Carrie and I were standin' by the fireplace warmin' our hands. I said, "Carrie, I've been thinkin' about something you said one time."

"What?" Carrie asked.

"You said you wished you knew how to handle horses as good as me," I said.

"Uh-huh," said Carrie.

"And I wish I knew how to read as good as you," I responded. "Do you want to swap lessons while we're here in Dundee?"

"That's a good idea, Luther. Let's do that."

Carrie walked across the kitchen and whispered something to Mrs. Pinkerton. She nodded and said, "I'll buy what you want next time I go shopping."

Carrie came back over to me and said, "Let's not start on the readin' lessons right away until Mrs. Pinkerton can go shoppin'."

"All right," I said. "We can start with the horses first."

We went out to the stables every day before and after work. The first thing I taught Carrie was the names for the different parts of a horse: the mane, the flank, the muzzle, and so on. Next I taught her how to water, feed, and groom the animals. She seemed interested in those things, but one mornin' she grabbed my arm and said, "Luther, what I really want is to learn how to *ride* a horse."

"Carrie," I told her, "I'm not tryin' to be mean by savin' the best for last, but you really need to understand horses before you can start ridin' them. I think you're about ready to start your ridin' lessons now."

Carrie caught on real quick when I showed her how to get on and off a horse, how to balance, and how to hold the reins. It wasn't long before she was a very good rider.

By that time Mrs. Pinkerton had gone shoppin' and brought us back some things to help with the readin' lessons. Evenin's after supper it was Carrie's turn to teach and my turn to learn. I expected her to use a book to give me lessons. Instead, she wrote one word on the slate that Mrs. Pinkerton bought. I looked at the word and asked Carrie, "What's that say?"

"Those letters spell *Luther*. This is how your name looks in print."

"Really!" I was so happy. I took my finger and slowly traced each letter. Carrie told me what to call each one as I traced. "That's an *L*, a *U*, a *T*, an *H*, an *E*, and an *R*." When she got to the last letter I pointed to each letter and said, "*L? U? T? H? E? R?*" Carrie grabbed my arm and said, "Yes, Luther, you're goin' to learn real fast." I smiled at her, then traced each letter again and again, until finally Mrs. Pinkerton said, "It's getting pretty late . . ." I hated to stop tracin', but I knew we had to get up early the next mornin'. Anyway, by the time Mrs. Pinkerton said it was late, I had already learned how to read and write my own name.

I dreamed about the word "Luther" every night. I practiced my name every chance I got. I took a twig and scratched the letters in the clay floor in the stable or dipped my fingers in the horse trough and tried writin' them on the stall before the water dried.

At the next lesson, Carrie handed me the slate and said, "Draw a horse."

"Girl, I don't want drawin' lessons. I want readin' lessons."

"I know, but draw a horse anyway."

"I don't see what drawin' a horse has to do with readin'." But I drew it anyway.

Carrie pointed to the mane I drew. She asked, "What's that?"

"It's a mane. You know I taught you that. Why are you askin' me questions about horses when you're supposed to be teachin' me to read?"

Instead of answerin', Carrie wrote the word "mane" on my horse picture. She did the same thing with the other parts of the horse. Finally she stopped writin' long enough to explain. "This is how the words you taught me look in print. You can tell which word is which by where they're written on the picture."

Well, with the pictures to look at, I soon knew how to read all those horse words, and before long I was readin' from Carrie's books.

About the middle of March, word came from Mr. Jones that the river between the United States and Canada was open again, and that he had arranged for us to take the Michigan Central Railroad from Chicago to Detroit.

Mr. Pinkerton took us back to the city in his carriage. Instead of takin' us to the Jones's house, he drove us to Mr. Jones's shop in the Sherman House Hotel on Clark Street. We waited in the back room, but we could see people comin' in and out. At closin' time, Mr. Jones took us to meet Mr. Isbell, a black barber who also had his shop in the hotel. "Mr. Isbell is another person who has helped people run away from slavery," he explained.

I don't know what made me ask this, but I said, "Mr. Isbell, did you ever help a man named Harvey Lee and a woman named Emma? They were from Missouri and had a little girl named Dilly with them. They're our family."

Mr. Isbell was polishin' his barberin' tools so they'd be ready for the next mornin'. He didn't answer my question right away. Instead, he dropped his scissors as if they were hot coals, and quickly asked Mr. Jones to step out of the barbershop into the hallway of the hotel.

Carrie and I wondered why. When the two men came back in, they told us to sit down. The chairs were red velvet and I would have felt pretty important sittin' in one if it hadn't been for the look on Mr. Isbell's face.

He got a chair for himself and one for Mr. Jones and brought them over to Carrie and me. Mr. Jones spoke first. "Mr. Isbell has just told me some news about your parents." Mr. Isbell picked up where Mr. Jones left off. "I met your parents and arranged for them to take a tall sailing ship to Canada. Captain Blake is an abolitionist and agreed to take them around Lake Michigan and to a safe port in Canada."

Carrie and I were so happy we almost fell out of our fancy chairs huggin' each other.

After our meetin' with Mr. Isbell, we climbed into Mr. Jones's carriage and passed in front of a big, beautiful buildin'. John Jones said, "I wanted you to see this magnificent railway station. I hope someday you can walk in here and buy a train ticket to any city you wish to visit. But it would be too dangerous to do that now." He explained we were to ride in the baggage car so that we wouldn't run the risk of bein' seen by slave catchers.

Mr. Jones took us to the train yards. He pointed to the baggage car we were supposed to get on and told us good-bye.

We climbed into the car and smoothed our blankets out behind some trunks and shippin' crates.

Before long the train started, and we were on our way. Lyin' there listenin' to the wheels rollin' toward Detroit and Canada, I got to wonderin', What was life goin' to be like in Canada? How could Carrie and I earn a livin'? Would we have to go to different cities to find work? Would we lose track of each other? Carrie must have been thinkin' the same thing. She said, "Luther, what are we goin' to do when we get to Canada?"

"I don't know."

"You think we'll be able to stay together and support ourselves?"

"I don't know, but remember soon after our family escaped, Daddy and Mama were talkin' about havin' to cross the Mississippi River?"

"Yeah, what about it?"

"They didn't know if we'd be able to get across, but remember what Daddy said, 'We'll find some way to cross it.'"

Carrie kind of laughed. "I remember him sayin' that, and we *did* get 'cross the Mississippi River."

"Sure did."

"I hope this time everything will work out all right for us."

"Me, too." I was beginnin' to feel sleepy. Carrie must have been sleepy, too, 'cause she yawned and said, "Good night, Luther."

We were able to sleep as long as the train was movin'. But every time the train stopped, we woke up and peeked through the cracks in the baggage car. We saw signs lit by lamps at each station tellin' the name of the town. I felt so proud that Carrie and I could both read: Niles, Kalamazoo, Battle Creek, Jackson, Ann Arbor, and DETROIT.

CHAPTER

12

It was night when we got to Detroit. We didn't know what to expect, so we hid behind some large crates in the baggage car. Someone slid the doors open, then two muscular men climbed in. They started takin' out trunks and crates. They put them in a little wagon they'd rolled up to the doors. Then they took away the first load. As soon as they left, a light-skinned black man stepped through the slidin' doors and whispered, "Quick, come with me." We followed him to his buggy. He told us his name was George DeBaptiste. He took us to the Second Baptist Church.

We went down to the basement. There were more black people in that room than I had ever seen. Some were standin'. Some were sittin'. Some were walkin' around. Others were stretched out on plank benches. They were tall and short, skinny and fat, young and old, dark and light, smilin' and sad. Some were doctorin' their swollen feet. Others were missin' fingers or had lash marks worse than those on Carrie's back. Several men had heavy pieces of iron shackled to their arms or feet. One man wore a horrible collar with spikes stickin' out so he could never lay down to rest.

Mr. DeBaptiste explained that many Underground Railroad routes from a lot of states led to Detroit. The people here had escaped from slavery and were waitin' for a boat to take 'em to Canada. Everyone seemed both happy and restless at the same time 'cause there was still a risk slave catchers could find 'em here, even this close to freedom, and force 'em back into slavery.

It was a strange feelin' to be in the midst of so many people and not see anyone we knew.

Carrie nudged me. "Doesn't that lady over there remind you of Mama?"

She sure did, except that her hair was gray and she had wrinkles when she smiled.

"There's space beside her. Do you want to go sit by her?" I asked.

"Sure. Why not?"

The lady gave us a welcomin' look as she saw us

comin' toward her. She began talkin' right away. "Hello, my name is Christina."

We told her our names. I asked where she had come from.

"I came here from Virginia. Walked almost all the way. Where'd you come from?"

"We came from Missouri," said Carrie.

"Really?" she asked. "Is St. Louis in Missouri?"

"Yes, ma'am, I'm pretty sure it is from what Mama used to say," Carrie answered.

"Well," the woman went on, "last I heard of my baby sister, they were takin' her to be sold at the St. Louis slave market. She could have been sold down to Louisiana or anywhere. I don't know whatever happened to her."

Carrie and I looked at each other. "Mama told us Cap'n bought her and Daddy in St. Louis," I said.

"And she and Daddy were both from Virginia," added Carrie.

"Really? What county?" the woman asked in kind of a desperate way.

"Mama never told us."

"What does your mama look like?" The woman was soundin' more and more excited.

Carrie said, "She looks a whole lot like you. In fact, that's why we happened to come sit by you."

"Really?" Now the lady almost gasped. "What's your mama's name?"

"It used to be Emma Spurlark. Now she's Emma Lawson." We had hardly finished talkin' when the woman threw her arms around us and gave us both a big hug!

"I am your auntie, Christina! My maiden name was Spurlark. Your mama is my long-lost baby sister!" Then she stood up and looked around the room. She asked us, "Where's Emma now?"

We went from the thrill of findin' our aunt to the sadness of knowin' that we might have lost Mama forever. We told Aunt Christina how our family escaped and got as far as Quincy, Illinois. And how last we heard Mama and Daddy were on a boat to Canada.

Aunt Christina shook her head. "You know, I had ten brothers and sisters and don't know where a one of them is now! Goodness only knows what's become of them. Slavery tears families to shreds."

Carrie and I continued tellin' what happened to our family. "We thought we could all stay together once we escaped, but after we crossed the Mississippi River some Underground Railroad people said it was safer for us to split up. Mama and them are probably in Canada right now."

We all sat quietly for awhile.

Aunt Christina put her arm around Carrie and me. Drawin' us close, she said, "I'm sure glad I found the two of you. You can come to Canada with us, and we can all go lookin' for your ma and pa."

I heard Aunt Christina say the word "us," but it was only when a man rushed over and kissed her that we realized Aunt Christina was not travelin' alone. The man looked and sounded happy when he said, "I have good news, Christina. If we go to a place called Buxton in Canada West, we can buy us a farm and have us a weddin'."

Aunt Christina smiled and squeezed the man's hand. She said, "That's wonderful, Edward." Then she told the man she'd called Edward, "I have even more good news. While you were gone to ask about places in Canada, I found a niece and nephew of mine."

She introduced us. "Edward, this is Carrie and this is Luther. They are my sister Emma's children from Missouri. They escaped with their parents but their family got split up. Luther and Carrie, this is my husband—and your uncle Edward Newman. We ran off when his massa went broke. We were 'fraid he'd be sold."

" 'Ello, Luther, 'Ello, Carrie," said Uncle Edward. "The two of you are a godsend. Christina and I never had any younguns of our own, but always wished we did. Y'all can be our younguns till you find your folks."

Carrie and I blurted out our thoughts. "Thank

you!" I said. "I can't tell you how glad I am that we met up with kinfolks."

Carrie cut in: "We didn't know what we'd do, or if the two of us would be split up, or . . ."

"You know, fate is funny," said Uncle Edward. "Just a few minutes ago the man who told me about Buxton said they have real good schools up there. I half-listened to that part of what he said, 'cause I never thought we'd have any younguns to be sendin' to school."

Aunt Christina was still smilin'. "I'm gettin' more excited than ever. How nice it will be to get to Canada and start our new life in the springtime. Now, we will have us a family—and on top of that we can do the two things we've always dreamed of."

"Buy us a farm and have a real weddin'!" exclaimed Uncle Edward.

"Your uncle Edward is a blacksmith, although he wants to try his hand at farmin'," said Aunt Christina. "But bein' a blacksmith he was able to hire himself out every Christmas and get paid for workin'. So he's got some money to buy a farm." Then she added, "We got married by jumpin' a broomstick, but that's slavery stuff. We want to get married like free folks do."

"We can help you with farmin' and the weddin'," I said.

"Oh, yes," cried Carrie. "I used to take care of the

chickens and work in the smokehouse and I'd love to help you get ready for the weddin'."

Just then, a tall, dark man with silver gray hair stepped into the room. Everybody stopped what they were doin' and looked at him.

Carrie nudged me and whispered, "Doesn't he look like an African king?"

The word "African" reminded me of the one African thing I had. I felt in my pocket and brought out the mramnuo Daddy had given me before our family escaped. I whispered to Carrie, "Don't you 'spose Daddy's father looked like that man standin' there?"

In my side vision I could see Carrie noddin' her head yes. But I couldn't look straight at her; I was too busy lookin' at the eyes of the man standin' in the doorway. He looked as if he could see right into the souls of everybody in that room.

Uncle Edward leaned over and whispered, "That's Mr. William Lambert. He's the one who told me about goin' to Buxton."

In a low voice, Aunt Christina added, "We heard somebody say Mr. Lambert is head of a secret order. And that he's friends with a man named John Brown."

"I wonder if that's the same John Brown that Mama said Cap'n and the other Missouri planters used to be talkin' about while she was servin' dinner," mused Carrie.

We all hushed when Mr. Lambert spoke. In a deep, rich voice he said, "May I have your attention!" He was quiet for a minute, then announced, "We will have boats leaving for Canada all through the night. Although there are would-be slave catchers here in Detroit and you are still in danger, if all goes well, you will have crossed the river to Canada by sunrise tomorrow."

My heart thumped with excitement when I heard Mr. Lambert say, "Canada" and "tomorrow."

It was just after midnight when we huddled into wagons out back of Second Baptist Church. Somebody said the wagon wheels were padded and the horses' hooves were covered to muffle any sound. I know one thing for sure, the horses and the wagons were really quiet goin' down the street.

The wagons stopped when we got to the wharf. Without a sound we climbed out and walked toward the boats. I looked around me. It was so dark you could only see the outlines of people movin'.

Mr. Lambert had warned us the Detroit River was as deep as it was wide. The water was as black as pitch. I could hear it lap against our boat. It was not frozen solid, but there were large chunks of ice floatin' on the surface. If anyone, heaven forbid, should fall overboard, they could never be fished out.

Uncle Edward and Aunt Christina told Carrie and me to stay between 'em. Aunt Christina whispered, "We can't take a chance on losin' you two."

Carrie whispered back, "It feels good to be in a family again." I was thinkin' the same thing. I was surprised the boat was so big. I had expected a little canoe. In the darkness, the boat looked about as big as the baggage car we rode comin' into Detroit.

We climbed on board. We couldn't find four seats together, but Carrie and Aunt Christina found seats near the front.

Uncle Edward and I walked farther back and found some seats there. He said, "I overheard somebody describin' this as an excursion boat. And that it's owned by a black man named George DeBaptiste."

I almost forgot to whisper. "George DeBaptiste! He's the man who met Carrie and me at the train station in Detroit."

From where I was sittin', I could see the outline of a man pull up the anchor and soon we were steamin' toward Canada.

CHAPTER

13

The sky was dark. When I looked up, the moon was almost hidden by charcoal clouds. I'd never seen the moon look quite like that before. It was as if it understood that we had to cross over and wasn't goin' to expose us to unfriendly eyes.

Next thing I knew, the water was lappin' against huge rocks. The boat was tied up on the Canadian shore, and the strong, kind, outstretched hands of black and Indian and white people were there to welcome us and guide us ashore.

The first thing many people did when they stepped off the boat was kneel and pray. Others kissed the ground.

Uncle Edward, Aunt Christina, Carrie, and I

prayed and kissed the ground, both. In our prayer we said we hoped the rest of our family was safe and that we could find them.

As we stood up a man stepped out of the shadows and said, "Mr. Lambert has sent word that you wish to go to the Buxton Settlement. Please follow me to my wagon."

We did as the man said, although he hadn't told us his name or how he knew about us. Carrie and I climbed up and sat on the front seat next to the driver.

Aunt Christina and Uncle Edward sat on bales of hay in the back of the wagon. Our aunt leaned forward and gave Carrie and me a pat on the shoulder. Our uncle leaned forward so he could see, since part of the wagon was blockin' his view. "We're leavin' the river and headin' inland," he said. "I'm glad 'cause if I was to stay here in this town, I'd always be worried some slave catcher might sneak up on me."

"Some people risk stayin' here for one reason or another, but you can breathe a little easier in Buxton," said the driver.

"How far is Buxton?" I asked.

"Eighty or ninety kilometers from here," he answered.

"How long does it take to get there?" asked Carrie.

"About twenty-four hours," he said. "If slave

catchers tried to follow you that far, most likely they'd get lost."

The sun was beginnin' to come up. I could just barely see the outlines of the buildin's. But the buildin's were so close together, I figured we were passin' through a city.

I asked the driver, "Where are we now?"

"This is Windsor, Ontario."

"Ontario? I thought we were in Canada," exclaimed Carrie.

"Ontario is in Canada."

"You had me worried for a minute," said Carrie.

"Is there a place called London around here?" I asked. "That's where we think our parents are."

"There is a place called London, but it's not around here," said our driver. "It's farther inland than the Buxton Settlement, where I'm taking you."

The driver had been nice about answerin' our questions, so I got up the nerve to ask him about something else. "You knew who we were when we got off the boat. What's your name?" I could tell he was surprised at me askin' that question, 'cause he tightened the reins and the horse jolted.

He cleared his throat and said, "They call me 'Guinea Jim.' " Then, as if he wanted to change the subject, he started pointin' out the sights along the way, although it was hard to see much in the early dawn light.

"This is the train station, and it's almost time for the mornin' train."

I looked over as our wagon rolled by. I could see the shape of a big buildin'. Gaslights lit up the train platform. Black people and white people were standin' side by side. A livery was hitched to a post. I could see the outline of the driver standin' and talkin' to his horse like Daddy and I used to do when we were tendin' to Cap'n's horses.

Bein' around horses was the one thing I missed about the plantation. I got to thinkin' about the farm Uncle Edward wanted to buy. I was hopin' he could get a farm real soon so I could tend to horses again.

We'd gone way past the station when I thought how much that livery driver had reminded me of Daddy. I figured he was on my mind because I was wishin' so much that we could find him and Mama and Dilly.

The sun was gettin' higher and higher in the sky. Guinea Jim told Carrie and me, "You better go get inside the wagon now that the sun's comin' up."

That was fine with me. I was gettin' drowsier and drowsier. The night before I'd been so excited about crossin' the river to Canada, I had hardly blinked much less slept. Now sleep was comin' down on me.

14

We jostled along in the wagon all day. It was rough goin'. The road was bumpy. Part of the time we took trails that were even bumpier. Bushes and trees grew right up to the edge of the trails.

Toward evenin' Guinea Jim stopped at a stream that was in the thick woods. Instead of callin' 'em woods, he said, "We'll stop here in the Bushland."

He made a campfire. Then he reached in back of his wagon and took out an iron cookin' pot. He had some things stored in the pot includin' flour, one-quart canning jars, cornmeal, and a black skillet. He emptied what was in the jars into the cookin' pot and stirred up a batch of corn cakes. Before long we were sittin' around the fire eatin' some good-tastin' stew and hotcakes.

"When folks at that church in Detroit talked about Buxton Settlement," said Uncle Edward, "they told me it was started by a white preacher named Reverend King. He was from Louisiana. He married a woman who owned slaves, but as soon as she died, he came to Canada. He bought land and divvied it up into farms. Thanks to him, folks who had been slaves got to be first-class citizens."

I was listenin' and watchin' the campfire at the same time. Without realizin' it, I yawned out loud. I said, "Scuse me." I didn't want Guinea Jim to think I was bored.

He knew we'd had a long day. He had, too, so he said, "That's enough talk for one night. There are bears and wolves in the bush. You'll need to sleep in the wagon. I'll stretch out on the front seat."

"Guinea Jim, will you tell us more about Buxton tomorrow?" Carrie asked sleepily.

"Yes," he answered. His voice was beginnin' to sound sleepy, too. "Here are some blankets for you."

I took one and curled up in a corner of the wagon. Even with bears and wolves around that night, I felt safer than I'd ever felt before.

I was up early the next mornin', rested and rarin' to go. I helped Guinea Jim hitch his team of horses to the wagon. "Last night we heard about how

Buxton Settlement got started. What's it goin' to be like there?" I asked.

"Good. Very good," he answered.

"How? What do you mean?"

"It has a church and a school."

Carrie sat up in the wagon. "Did you hear that, Luther? We can go to school."

"It's such a good school that black and white folk from all around send their children to it," Guinea Jim explained.

Uncle Edward and Aunt Christina had been sittin' in the wagon listenin' to all this, too. My uncle said, "Is Buxton just farmland? Or are there some businesses there, too?"

"It's quite built up," answered Guinea Jim. "There's a post office, brickyard, sawmill, bank, and even a two-story hotel. And they're all run by black folks."

"I can't wait to get there," said Aunt Christina.

"You're goin' to one of the best places in Canada. There's no slavery in this country, but it's got its share of racial problems," said Guinea Jim.

"So Mr. Lambert sent us to Buxton Settlement because it's one of the better places in Canada," said Uncle Edward.

"Yep," answered Guinea Jim.

It seemed like even the horse wanted to hurry up and reach the Buxton Settlement. He trotted along without gettin' tired.

We got there two days and a night after we'd stepped on the free soil of Canada. We didn't expect anybody to take notice of us when we rode up in Guinea Jim's wagon. To our surprise, the townspeople greeted us by ringin' the town's Liberty Bell.

Carrie and I had seen other towns as we'd made our escape. We'd even seen the big cities of Chicago, Illinois, and Windsor, Canada, but Buxton Settlement was the best town we'd *ever* seen.

While we were lookin' all around, Uncle Edward and Aunt Christina climbed down from Guinea Jim's wagon and started to ask people on the street about buyin' land. Someone told them about a farm that was for sale.

My aunt and uncle came back to the wagon. Uncle Edward said, "That farm sounds like just what we've been wishin' for."

"It sure does!" exclaimed Aunt Christina.

"I didn't know that farm was up for sale," said Guinea Jim. "It's been a while since I was in Buxton. But it's a nice piece of property and I know the owner. Would you like to meet him?"

"Yes," said my aunt and uncle.

"I think we can get out there by nightfall. It's near where we'll be stoppin'."

"Thank you."

It was dark by the time we got to the farm. The owner was a man whose wife had recently died. He was in poor health and wanted to sell the farm and go live with his married children. He took a likin' to us.

He told Uncle Edward and Aunt Christina, "I'll be happy if my farm goes to a nice family like yours. I'm sure you'll enjoy it as much as my wife and I did." He reached into a drawer and pulled out some rolled-up papers with drawin's on them. He said, "It's too late to show you around outside, but these drawings will give you an idea of what the property is like."

My aunt and uncle looked at the drawin's. They whispered to each other and smiled. The next thing I knew Uncle Edward was shakin' hands with the man and sayin', "You have a sale."

Even Guinea Jim, who was usually serious, smiled. He took us to a little house on the edge of town. There were no lights on inside. He just opened the door and walked in. He told us, "You can stay here as long as you need to."

I wondered how Guinea Jim knew it was all right for us to stay in this deserted house. I asked, "Why isn't anybody home?"

Guinea Jim explained, "This is my house, but I'm usually travelin'."

We stayed at Guinea Jim's house a few days. Then one mornin' he announced, "The farm deed is ready for signin'."

After breakfast we went to an office in town. The man who was sellin' the farm was there. He and

Uncle Edward sat down at a desk with another man. They all looked at a paper that was on top of the desk, then the man sellin' the farm picked up an ink pen and wrote his name on the paper.

Carrie and I looked on. It was a magic moment. Aunt Christina stood beside Uncle Edward. He marked somethin' on the paper and then handed the pen to Aunt Christina. Neither one of them knew how to write their names, so they each made an *X* on the deed with great pride. Uncle Edward's hands were tremblin' and he splattered tears of joy as he counted out his hard-earned money to make his first payment on the farm.

Unlike most former slaves, Uncle Edward was able to pay the whole $12.50 for the first year in cash money. He marked another *X* on the deed, promisin' to finish payin' for the farm within the next nine years.

It was early spring 1856 when we took up land just outside the boundaries of the Buxton Settlement. Uncle Edward and Aunt Christina were lucky to be able to find a farm with a log cabin, a good well, and enough of the fifty acres of land cleared so we could start farmin' right away. The only drawback was the railroad tracks that cut through our land. They could bring trouble. Aunt Christina warned, "We'll always have to be on the lookout for trains."

Uncle Edward said, "We can protect ourselves by being careful, but there's no way to protect our fields from the sparks that fly out of the steam engine."

"Oh, Edward, stop worryin'. Let's just enjoy our new home," said Aunt Christina.

The house was set back from the road. It had a porch and flower garden in front and a picket fence between the house and the yard.

Neighbors from nearby farms came to welcome us and offer their help if we wanted anything. We thanked them and told 'em if they ever needed us to give 'em a hand, they could count on us, too.

Uncle Edward couldn't get over the good fortune of havin' such nice neighbors and a farm that was ready to work. "This is even better than I could have hoped for," he said.

Aunt Christina put her arm around his waist and said, "Now all we got to do is make marryin' plans."

"What'd you say?" asked a neighbor lady.

Aunt Christina told how she and my uncle had jumped the broom in slavery times and how she always dreamed of havin' a *real* weddin'. She explained, "It'll make me feel like I am really free."

All the neighbors understood and wanted to help make it the best weddin' ever. Most of them had been in slavery, too.

One man said, "I'll roast a pig." A lady who was a seamstress said, "I'll make your trousseau."

Carrie asked, "What's a true-so?"

The lady explained: "It's a set of fancy clothes for a bride."

Aunt Christina blushed and said, "Thank you, that's so sweet. You all make me feel like a princess."

Uncle Edward put his arm around my aunt and told her: "You deserve it. Our neighbors have just met you and they already see what a special lady you are, Christina." Then he said to the neighbors, "We want everyone to join us on our weddin' day."

"You'll have to get married in the yard then, 'cause there are eight hundred folk in this town," said the seamstress. Someone else added, "All the folks in nearby settlements will want to come, too."

"Oh, that will be so romantic," said Carrie. (I figured she must have learned that romantic word from some book she'd read.)

"I like the idea of gettin' married outdoors," said Aunt Christina. Glancin' around the yard she said, "I wonder where we could stand to take our vows?"

I glanced around, too, and thought of an idea. "I could build an arch over by the garden for you and Uncle Edward to stand under."

"Luther, that would be beautiful."

"And I'll make a flower crown for you to wear," said Carrie.

"Carrie, that would make me feel even more like a princess than I already do."

Uncle Edward had been quiet for awhile. He'd

been thinkin' ahead to the weddin'. "I wonder what preacher we can get to marry us," he said.

"Ask Reverend Josiah Henson," suggested a man standin' nearby. "He's in charge of the Dawn Settlement not far from here." All the other neighbors agreed that Reverend Henson would be a perfect choice.

Uncle Edward asked how to get in touch with Reverend Henson. "The sooner we can talk with him, the better," he said.

"I'll be goin' over to Dawn and will tell him you want to talk with him," said the man.

In the meantime Uncle Edward said, "Let's try our hands at farmin'." The neighbors loaned us a team of horses. Carrie and I planted a vegetable garden just outside the kitchen door. And we helped Aunt Christina and Uncle Edward plow and do everything else we knew to do to get the farm goin'. Havin' the weddin' to look forward to made our work seem easy.

Carrie and I often talked about how much we wished we could find our parents and Dilly in time for the weddin.' But we didn't mention this in front of Aunt Christina and Uncle Edward. They seemed so happy, we didn't want to take away from their happiness.

Everything seemed to be workin' out just fine for the weddin' and with the farmin', but one night

after supper, Aunt Christina started cryin.' Naturally, Uncle Edward asked, "What's the matter?"

"I just don't feel right makin' plans for a weddin' instead of goin' to look for my baby sister Emma and the rest of her family."

"I've been thinkin' about the same thing," said Uncle Edward. "Carrie and Luther think their daddy was plannin' to go to London, Ontario. Talkin' to the neighbors, I hear London's not too far from here. Let's hitch up the wagon and go up to London this comin' Saturday to see if we can find 'em."

"I hope we'll have as good a luck findin' our family as we had findin' this farm," said Aunt Christina.

All week the only thing we talked about was the trip. None of us had ever been to London, but Uncle Edward asked around Buxton Settlement about places in London where he might find somebody like Daddy who worked with horses.

We were hopeful when we loaded the wagon and set out first thing Saturday mornin'. It was a long hard ride to London. When we got there we asked everybody and looked everywhere we could tryin' to find the missin' part of our family.

We didn't have any luck. We were sadder than ever. Before we went lookin' we'd had high hopes. We were so disappointed now.

Carrie and I wanted to keep searchin'. So did

Aunt Christina. Finally Uncle Edward said, "Much as I hate to say this, we've got to get back to the farm. I asked a neighbor to take care of things for a few days, but we've got to return to Buxton soon."

"Can we come back to London again?" asked Carrie.

"Sure we can," answered Uncle Edward.

"Could we come back after harvesttime? Maybe we will think of other places to look by then," I said.

"That sounds like a good plan. In fact, if we don't find 'em next time, I promise you we'll come back each spring and fall for as long as you want," said Uncle Edward.

Aunt Christina didn't say anything. She was quieter than usual all the way home. Uncle Edward understood. He said, "Christina, I know how much you wanted to find your sister, and I hope we will find her someday. In the meantime, I know she would be glad that we are raisin' her children—and that she would want us to be happy."

Aunt Christina smiled and told him, "I hadn't thought of it that way."

When we got to Buxton we got word that Reverend Henson would be glad to marry my aunt and uncle and that he'd come over to talk with 'em ahead of time. That cheered us up some, but we were sad we hadn't found our parents.

We didn't have any time to waste, so we picked

up our lives where they'd left off before our trip. We worked on the farm and planned for the weddin'.

It was really goin' to be wonderful. Everything we made for that day had a special meanin' to us and was brand spankin' new.

Aunt Christina made herself a pretty weddin' dress. It was long and white with a high neck and puffy sleeves. She sewed rows and rows of lace and tiny little tucks on the front and wrists. It looked like it was made for a *real* princess.

Next Aunt Christina made Carrie's dress. Carrie sewed on some lace and hemmed it.

Carrie and I got out the little money we had saved from when we'd worked in Dundee. We couldn't think of any good thing to buy for our aunt and uncle, so we decided to just give them the money to use as they wished.

Meanwhile, my sister and I were workin' on other things. Carrie measured Aunt Christina's head size for a crown. She studied flowers in the garden and wildflowers on the farm to see which kinds of blossoms she wanted to use. Then she drew a little picture of the way she wanted to make the crown. She planned all the other flower decorations for the weddin', too.

I made an arch for the bride and groom to stand beneath while they were marryin'. Even the wood was special. It came from the Bushland on our farm. Uncle Edward took it to the sawmill in town to be cut. Then I built the arch. It was the first carpentry work I'd ever done, and I was pretty proud of the way it turned out.

CHAPTER

15

May 29, 1856, was a beautiful day in every way. The weddin' was the biggest and best get-together that had happened in a long time. The weather was perfect. Just the right temperature. Not a cloud in the sky.

Hundreds of people from miles around came in buggies, farm wagons, on horseback, and on foot. There were people from the Dawn and Buxton settlements and every place in between.

Reverend Josiah Henson was the first person to arrive. He was a dignified dark brown man with gray sideburns and a neatly trimmed beard. He talked with Uncle Edward and Aunt Christina. Then he asked Carrie and me to show him around the yard.

Some of the neighbors had made log benches. With the arch I'd finished and the rows of benches, the front yard looked like a church without walls.

Wild roses bloomed on the picket fence. It seemed like every flower in the garden was blossomin'. Carrie had put cut daisies in crocks. She even used the butter churn as a holder for a bunch of bright orange tiger lilies.

We filled a barrel to the brim with fresh-squeezed lemonade. It looked just like the barrels at Alan Pinkerton's shop that winter we'd spent in Dundee, Illinois. We wondered if maybe the barrels at the weddin' came from his shop.

There were long tables piled high with food. Former slaves who had escaped to Canada from different parts of the South brought their favorite dishes. There was everything from gumbo to squash pie. There was fried chicken, roast pig, and every kind of cake you could imagine.

Aunt Christina looked beautiful in the weddin' dress she had made and the flower crown Carrie had made for her. Uncle Edward looked happy and handsome in his Sunday suit.

Carrie was the maid of honor. I was the best man.

We stood under the arch as Reverend Henson said all the marryin' words, and a lady named Miss Rhue sang a song.

"I feel like I'm finally free," said Aunt Christina

after the ceremony. She started cryin' again, but this time she shed happy tears.

All the guests shook hands and hugged Aunt Christina and Uncle Edward. They seemed to be as happy as the bride and groom. The weddin' gave everybody a greater feelin' of hope and freedom.

The dinner bell rang. We went over to the tables and piled our plates high with food. We sat down. Everyone held hands and bowed heads as Reverend Henson blessed the food. After eatin', the grown-ups stood around laughin' and talkin'. Us young ones visited and played games. Carrie and I met some of our future classmates that day.

The guests had such a good time they stayed till early evenin'. Those that lived close by went home to feed their farm animals. Those that lived far away had made plans to stay overnight with relatives and friends.

Carrie and I took a pitcher of lemonade and some pound cake and sat on the front porch talkin' about the day. We were happy with the way everything had gone.

I said, "The only thing that would have made it better would have been . . ."

Carrie finished my sentence, ". . . if Mama, Daddy, and Dilly could have been there."

CHAPTER

16

With the weddin' over we turned our full attention to the farm. Uncle Edward had high hopes. He had been told by other farmers the soil around Buxton produced good crop yields and that the livestock thrived. He told Aunt Christina, "We should be independent in a few years."

A neighbor loaned us a little book called *Notes of Canada West*. He said the book was written by a young lady teacher whose family lived in Buxton. The young woman's name was Mary Ann Shadd. She had not only written a book, she was the editor of a newspaper.

Carrie and I were excited to see the book and to know it was written by somebody whose family lived near us. "I'm so proud," said Carrie. "I've seen a lot of books but I never saw one written by a woman before."

The neighbor said, "You can take double pride. Mary Ann Shadd is a young black woman."

Carrie hugged the book as she cried, "Really? I hope I can meet her someday!"

"So do I," I chimed in. (But to tell the truth I didn't know it was unusual for a black person or a woman of any race to write a book. Maybe I hadn't seen as many books as Carrie, but it seemed to me that anybody who lived in a free country should be free to write a book if they wanted to.)

Carrie still had the book in her arms when I said, "Will you stop huggin' that book long enough for us to see what's inside?"

"Oh, I'm sorry, Luther. I was just so happy, I forgot. . . ." She handed the book to me.

Notes of Canada West was the first book I'd held since Carrie had taught me to read. It was a thrill to see words printed on a page. And for me to be able to read 'em. It was the first time I could really understand why Carrie was so crazy about readin'.

The book was skinny, but it was full of information. It told everything a new farmer would need to know. It even told how many bushels you could grow on an acre. Carrie and I read every word of it. When we got through readin' the last

word on the last page, Aunt Christina said, "It does my heart good to see you children readin' like that."

"Well, what do you think we should plant?" asked Uncle Edward.

Carrie and I read off a real long list of crops and animals that could be raised in Canada West.

Our uncle held up his hand and said, "Stop. We can't grow *everything* on that list. Let's start with a few things, then maybe add somethin' else next year."

"I guess we got carried away," I muttered.

A week later, we bought two horses, some cows, and some chickens. Aunt Christina sounded proud when she said, "We have horses to pull the plow and the wagon, cows for milk, and chickens for eggs and eatin'."

"There's one more thing we might want to think about," said Uncle Edward. "Some people around town told me tobacco grows well here. They said former slaves brought tobacco to Canada and it brings a good price."

"Edward Newman, don't ever bring a tobacco plant near this farm," scolded my aunt. "I have spent too many days of my life workin' tobacco—primin' it, tyin' it—you name it and I've done it. You and the children can grow anything you want, just not tobacco," she added. "I want nothin' more to do with fieldwork. I just want to enjoy my kitchen and my chickens."

"I didn't know you felt so strong about tobacco," said my uncle. "I know you've done too many years of backbreakin' fieldwork. I promised you a long time ago if we bought a farm I would never ask you to come out in the field."

After Aunt Christina had made it very clear that we were not goin' to grow tobacco, we got back to decidin' what we *were* goin' to do.

Carrie and I asked Uncle Edward if he'd let us train the horses. He said, "Sure. And if you do that they can be yours." We were *so* happy! We had never dreamed we'd ever own horses! Later Carrie said, "Luther, I sure am glad you taught me to work with horses," and I told her, "And I'm sure glad you taught me to read."

Durin' the summer, the tomatoes, cucumbers, and beans were always ready to pick. When Carrie and I were in the garden we felt as carefree as the little white butterflies that flitted around the cabbage plants.

In addition to vegetables, different kinds of fruit were always in season. Some kinds were wild. Others had been planted by the folks who had lived on the farm before us. Strawberries, mulberries, raspberries, blackberries, grapes, cherries, apples, plums, and pears. Carrie and I had the best time pickin'. Truth be told, Carrie and I ate as much fruit as we took into the house.

Aunt Christina loved her kitchen, and although she was a sharin' person, she didn't want anybody "meddlin' " in there. She refused to let anyone help her as she made delicious jams, jellies, and pies. She canned lots of the fruit so we could enjoy it all winter.

Carrie and I did all kinds of jobs around the farm. Aunt Christina and Uncle Edward had been so nice to us—and they were kind of gettin' up in age. We wanted to do everything we could to help. After all, we were all family and the farm was our home now.

At six each mornin', we drew water and carried it to the troughs. We toted a lot of water, since a horse drinks around twenty gallons a day. We groomed the horses and fed 'em hay, oats, barley, and molasses. (The molasses kept the dust down on the oats—and horses love sweet things.) Next we cleaned out the stalls. In warm weather we wiped down the horses' legs with fly wipe. Then we put 'em out to pasture so they could get sun and exercise. We made sure there was enough water in the trough in the pasture for 'em to drink durin' the day. About six in the evenin', we fed 'em. Later we took 'em back to their stalls in the barn. Each week we cleaned the harnesses with saddle soap. I must've been a pretty good teacher, 'cause Carrie really knew how to handle horses.

I named my horse Sugar and Carrie named hers Spice. Trainin' them took a lot of time and work. But it was fun. First, we got the horses used to havin' a bridle in their mouth. Second, we taught them to go left or right. Third, we got them used to our weight. Fourth, we got them used to doin' all these things at once. Our horses were smart and were pretty well trained in about five months. Some horses take a year to train.

After the day's work was done Carrie and I went bareback ridin' in and around Buxton.

The farm was runnin' pretty smoothly by the time school opened.

Carrie was thrilled about goin' to school. "I'm sure glad I don't have to worry about somebody like Cap'n whippin' me . . . for tryin' to learn."

Although I hadn't said much, I was lookin' forward to goin' to school, too.

Each mornin', after we took care of the horses, did our other chores, and ate breakfast, we walked three miles to a log church–schoolhouse with rough-hewn benches and tables.

Our teacher's name was Mr. John Rennie. We not only learned readin' and writin' and 'rithmetic, but we learned geography, music, and languages like Greek and Latin, too.

The year we started school, there were six older students who were ready for college. One of them, James P. Rapier, grew up and went on to the Congress of the United States.

Naturally, Carrie and I enjoyed goin' to school, meetin' our teacher and classmates, and bein' able to read any book we wanted. But we weren't the only ones from our house who were goin' to school. Aunt Christina and Uncle Edward were goin' to night school. Even though they were grown and knew so many things, they had never even had a chance to learn their ABC's. They stayed up late, readin' by the light from the oil lamp on the kitchen table.

All was well except for the naggin' question: What had happened to our parents and Dilly?

One evenin' shortly before harvesttime, Uncle Edward came in from the fields and said, "Christina, Luther, and Carrie, we're goin' to have a good crop. Not bad for first-time farmers, if I do say so myself."

The harvest was even better than Uncle Edward had expected. Carrie wrote down the total yields. Carrie and I helped as Uncle Edward read some of Carrie's notes out loud: "Thirty bushels of wheat per acre. Forty bushels of barley. Seventy bushels of oats. I'm glad you kept such good records, Carrie. We should plant the same crops next year, and maybe add one more. In the meantime, we should be able to get a good price for the wheat."

"Instead of addin' another crop, what would you think of us gettin' more horses?" I asked. "Carrie and I could train 'em. Seems like we could make a tidy profit if we raised 'em and sold 'em."

"That sounds like a good idea," said Uncle Edward.

"You already know I learned a lot about horses from bein' around my daddy 'fore he was sold. After bein' sold, he came back to Cap'n's where Mama, Carrie, Dilly, and I stayed. On one trip he gave me this." I held out my hand with the mramnuo. "Daddy said his daddy—who was my grand-daddy—used to work with horses in Africa. So I guess bein' good with horses got handed down through the family."

Uncle Edward smiled as he looked at my little statue, but he didn't say anything for a minute. Then he told me: "Luther, hearin' your idea makes me think of somethin'. . . . You know I'm a black-smith by trade. . . . I enjoy farmin', but to be hon-est, I kind of miss bein' a smith. Since my time is now my own, I don't see why I can't be both a farmer and a blacksmith." Uncle Edward told us his plan. "I think I might set up a blacksmith shop here on the farm. That way I could shoe our horses and maybe our neighbors would let me shoe their horses too."

"But, Edward, let's make another trip to London

before we do anything else. I want so much to try and find my sister and the rest of her family," said Aunt Christina.

"So do I," said Uncle Edward. "I haven't forgot the promise I made before the weddin'."

We went to London. We looked high and low for our family that fall and the followin' spring. We went back and looked some more the next fall and spring, too, but with no luck. Once or twice our hopes were raised when we met people who said they'd seen a man and woman that fit our description. But it always turned out those people couldn't give us a clue as to how to find that man and woman. Our hopes of findin' our missin' family got dimmer and dimmer.

Otherwise, Carrie and I were livin' a good life. In the fall we enjoyed gatherin' walnut, butternut, and hickory nuts in the woods. On cold winter evenin's we sat around the kitchen fireplace and roasted the nuts and ate 'em. Another thing we did in winter was go down to the lake when it froze to watch Uncle Edward and the neighbor men harvest big blocks of ice. Then we'd follow 'em to the icehouse. It was our job to cover the ice with sawdust to keep it from meltin'. If we did a good job, the ice would last for months and we would have ice for makin' ice cream and coolin' the milk house. The worst thing anybody could do was to make the mistake of leavin' the icehouse door open and lettin' all that precious ice melt. I scared myself once by almost doin' that, but something told me I'd better go back and check. Was I ever glad I went back and closed the door tight!

CHAPTER

17

Things were goin' real well with the farm, the horse trainin', and the blacksmith business.

Our crops were sellin' at a good price. Our neighbors put the word out that we had well-trained horses and that Uncle Edward was a good blacksmith.

One warm fall day in 1858 when Carrie and I came home from school, Aunt Christina greeted us with some news. She said, "Uncle Edward has a big surprise for you."

"What?" asked Carrie.

"Wait till Uncle Edward comes in for supper."

"Did he sell a horse?" I asked.

"No . . ."

"Will you give us a hint?" asked Carrie.

"No . . ."

"Let's go do our chores, Carrie," I said.

"Do your chores but don't go down to the black-smith shop pesterin' your uncle," said Aunt Christina.

After we finished our chores, Carrie and I got back for supper earlier than ever. When Uncle Edward stepped in the door, we ran up to him and begged him to tell us his surprise. He was in as much a teasin' mood as Aunt Christina. He seemed to enjoy keepin' us guessin'. He took longer than usual to wash up for supper.

Finally, he said, "I had a new customer at the blacksmith shop today."

"Really? Who?" asked Carrie.

"A man named Abraham Shadd."

"Abraham Shadd?" asked Carrie. "He's the father of Mary Ann Shadd, the woman who wrote *Notes of Canada West* . . ."

"And," I added, "the editor of the *Provincial Freeman* newspaper."

Uncle Edward smiled. "That's right."

"What did Mr. Shadd say?" I asked.

"Well, he asked me to shoe his horse," answered Uncle Edward. "And he said that his daughter, Mary Ann, is visitin' his house." He chuckled. "Mr. Shadd invited us to come over and meet her this evenin'."

Carrie let out a yell. *"Meet her?* Let's go right now! I'm not hungry. I'd rather meet Mary Ann Shadd than eat."

"Mr. Shadd said to come about eight so you'll have time to eat *and* meet his daughter," said Aunt Christina.

We gobbled down supper and got dressed to go. I hitched Sugar and Spice to the wagon and we set out.

Mr. and Mrs. Shadd made us feel real welcome. They invited us to sit in their front parlor and served our favorite treat, lemonade and pound cake.

Mary Ann Shadd was a tall, beautiful young woman who wore her hair pulled back from her face. She seemed as happy to meet Carrie and me as we were to meet her. She liked it when we told her we had read every word of her book and that it had helped our family a whole lot.

We asked her about runnin' a newspaper. She told us, "I have to write stories, have the type set, have the paper printed, and then sell it." We hadn't known how much work it was.

"When I grow up," said Carrie, "I hope I can be just like you—writin' books and writin' stories for newspapers."

"I hope you will," said Mary Ann Shadd, "but you don't have to be an author or an editor to express yourself through writing. In fact, you don't have to be grown to be a writer. Each of you should start keeping a daily journal right now. It's easy and fun. You simply write down what's happening in your life and how you feel about it."

"I don't have much time for writin'," I said. "I spend most of my time workin' with horses."

"Maybe you'd enjoy being a veterinarian when you grow up," said Mary Ann Shadd. "Then you could write for your own enjoyment in the evenings, rather than as a way to make a living."

"You said, 'veta-narian'?" I asked. I had never heard that word before.

"Yes. A veterinarian is an animal doctor. I'm sure with your love of horses, you'd be an excellent veterinarian. Your services would be very much in demand."

After she said that, she excused herself from the parlor. A few minutes later she came back with two blank ledger books. She gave one to Carrie and one to me. "Now write your name on the first page and today's date on the second page. Then when you get home write what you did today."

"I'm goin' to write that I met you," I said.

"I'm goin' to write down the very same thing, of course," said Carrie.

My sister and I were not the only ones impressed by Mary Ann Shadd. On the way home Uncle Edward commented, "I've met folks who did almost every kind of work you can think of, but I never met a writer before."

Aunt Christina said, "Me neither." Then she told Carrie and me, "Uncle Edward and I decided to use the money you gave us before the weddin' to buy a subscription to the *Provincial Freeman*. We figured that was somethin' we could all enjoy."

My uncle's blacksmith shop was a gatherin' place for the local menfolk. They came to get their horses shoed, and to tell and hear the latest news. When we weren't at school, Carrie and I found some excuse to hang around the shop so we could hear what was said. We sometimes took turns workin' the bellows to blow air on the fire in the forge.

My uncle and the customers often talked about politics. Any man aged twenty-one or more was eligible to vote if he had lived in Canada West three years and owned land. No woman in Canada or the United States could vote at that time.

Sometimes the talk would turn into long, loud, but friendly discussions about how wonderful it was that in Canada West, black men had the same rights as any other men and could be full-fledged citizens. Uncle Edward usually just listened when his customers got into these discussions, but one particular day, he couldn't keep quiet any longer. He argued, "Yes, it's good we men can have the vote, but it's not fair that women don't. Christina should have the same rights and privileges as me."

Carrie and I said, "Tell 'em, Uncle Edward." We kind of mumbled it to ourselves, though. We didn't want anybody to hear us and say we were too young to be overhearin' that kind of talk.

At dinner that night, Uncle Edward told Aunt Christina what he and his customers had discussed about the votin'. She was pleased when he told her he had argued that men and women should have the same rights.

"I agree," said Aunt Christina. "I wish more men felt like you do." She stopped talkin' for a minute, then announced, "I have an idea."

"What is it?" asked Uncle Edward.

"I'm goin' to invite the wives of your customers to meet me here in the kitchen. We can discuss politics and how we can start workin' toward gettin' the vote for women."

"Votin' can sure make a difference," said my uncle. "My customers take pride in tellin' me about how they got rid of a local member of Parliament who tried his best to ruin the Buxton Settlement."

Despite the talk of politics in the blacksmith shop, most days the discussions were about everyday news like who was diggin' a new well or had a bigger-than-usual crop.

All that changed in May of 1858 when a tall, bearded white man came to town. The man's name was John Brown, and he was something of a mystery man. The talk in the blacksmith shop was more excitin' than ever, but it was in quiet voices. Uncle Edward and his customers seemed to be watchin' and waitin' for something unusual to happen.

There was a rumor that John Brown had gone to see Reverend Josiah Henson, the preacher who had married Aunt Christina and Uncle Edward. There was another rumor that John Brown had even gone to—and maybe stayed at—the homes of some of Uncle Edward's customers, includin' Mary Ann Shadd's father and brother. It was whispered that John Brown was plannin' to have a meetin' the customers called a "Constitutional Convention," whatever that means.

One of Uncle Edward's customers was a doctor named Martin Delaney. He was the person all the other customers thought knew more about John Brown than he was tellin'.

Most of the time the customers went home at suppertime, but once John Brown came to town, they began to stay late into the night.

One evenin' a stranger appeared in the shadows outside the blacksmith shop. All the customers hushed. They had heard enough about John Brown to believe he was the man in the shadows. Uncle Edward walked outside to greet him. John Brown said, "I need six horses." Uncle Edward answered, "We'll get 'em for you." To our surprise, he motioned to Carrie and me and told us to go after them.

We dashed to the barn, bridled, and led all the horses—except Sugar and Spice—out of their stalls. We got back to the blacksmith shop in no time and gave Uncle Edward a what-should-we-do-now? kind of look. He motioned for us to hand the reins to John Brown. Havin' heard grown men talk about John Brown in whispers, I was really kind of scared to go right up to this mystery man. As I walked toward him, I thought I could see the fire from the blacksmith forge mirrored in his eyes. Never in all my life—includin' when Carrie and I were makin' our escape from slavery—had my heart beat so hard.

It turned out that I didn't need to be scared. When I got up close, John Brown's eyes didn't look fiery at all. Instead, he had a twinkle in his eye. He thanked Carrie and me for bringin' him the horses. As he took the reins, the horses fanned out to form a circle around the three of us. The reins were spread like spokes of a wheel and the horses stood where the rim of a wheel would be. Carrie, John Brown, and I were in the hub.

In a voice that sounded very kind—and very tired—John Brown told us, "I want you to know something. I will do everything in my power to see to it that *all* children experience the kind of freedom you have here in Buxton."

With that, he raised his hand and five men stepped

into view. John Brown and the men mounted the horses and rode away. As they left, they were joined by six more horsemen who'd been hidin' in the woods.

Carrie and I watched, spellbound. Finally, I was able to talk. "I'm sure glad we had those horses to give John Brown."

Carrie whispered, "Me, too. And I'm glad we got to see him up close."

18

Eighteen fifty-nine was not a good year. Everything seemed to go wrong.

One night at harvesttime I heard the clickety-clackin' of the train as it passed through our farmlands. I'd heard it so many nights before that I didn't pay it much mind. But then I heard a cracklin' sound and smelled smoke.

Just as Uncle Edward had feared, a spark from the engine had landed in our fields.

"Fire!" I yelled. "Wake up everybody. Our crops are burnin'!"

Uncle Edward, Aunt Christina, Carrie, and I all ran outdoors. Leapin' flames lit the sky as bright as day. Aunt Christina clanged the dinner bell to wake up the neighbors. The rest of us scooped water from the horse troughs and ran to fling water on the ragin' fire.

The neighbors came. They quickly filled and passed buckets of water along a line of people that led from the well to the fields, but there was no way the bucket brigade could pour on enough water to put out those flames. We stood and watched all our hard work go up in smoke.

We planted new crops in the spring of 1860, but our hearts weren't in it. We knew the same thing could happen again.

Carrie and I had finally realized that we weren't goin' to find Daddy, Mama, and Dilly anywhere around London. Aunt Christina and Uncle Edward had long since given up, but they kept takin' Carrie and me up there so we could look. We just didn't know anyplace else to go.

Our friend John Brown was hung in December of 1859 for his raid on Harpers Ferry, Virginia. There were lots of rumors sayin' the United States was goin' to have a war between the North and the South.

We were all just mopin' around. One night at supper Uncle Edward pushed his chair back from the table. "I think we should cheer ourselves up," he said. "I know we usually celebrate British Emancipation Day here in Buxton. I thought this year we might like to go to Amherstburg. I hear the people of Amherstburg march to the dock to greet folks from out of town, then the crowd parades back to a big park where they sing and eat and play games all day long."

"I think that would be wonderful," said Aunt Christina.

"So do I," said Carrie. "Emancipation Day is my favorite holiday."

"Freedom to everyone in the British Empire is somethin' to celebrate," I added.

"How will we get to Amherstburg?" asked Carrie.

"There is a mornin' train from Chatham to Windsor," said Uncle Edward. "We can get a livery to take us to catch a boat from Windsor to Amherstburg."

"That sounds like fun," I said.

We spent the summer of 1860 gettin' ready for Emancipation Day. We were surprised at how much we laughed and talked about our plans. Aunt Christina said, "This is the most special day since the weddin'!" Carrie asked Aunt Christina, "Will you help me make a new dress?"

We all began tellin' what we wanted to take with us. We each thought of so many things. I said, "We're goin' to need a trunk to carry our belongin's and lunch in." That gave Aunt Christina an idea—to put wheels on a small trunk we had. "I can do that," I said. Since makin' the arch for the weddin', I'd gotten interested in buildin' things.

The trunk turned out really well. It was lightweight enough to pick up and put on the train. We could also roll it instead of carryin' it.

Emancipation Day couldn't come fast enough to suit us. Carrie and I crossed the days off the calendar and counted to see how many were left.

At last it was July 31, the night before Emancipation Day. By the time Carrie and I went out to do our nightly chores, we had most of our lunch packed. We put the fried chicken, biscuits, apple butter, cake, pies, some fresh picked plums, and a ham in the icehouse to keep cool overnight. We had our best clothes all laid out and ready to put on. Aunt Christina told us to get some sleep before train time, but I was much too excited. I tried to stay awake so I could be sure nobody else overslept.

At midnight I told everybody, "Wake up. It's Emancipation Day!" Carrie was half asleep when she stumbled through the house wishin' everybody a happy Emancipation Day.

We all washed up in icy-cold water. This was one mornin' we couldn't take time to make a fire in the woodstove and heat the water. Carrie and I went out to the icehouse and got the food.

We ate some biscuits and sliced ham for our breakfast. We checked to make sure we weren't forgettin' anythin'. Pretty soon we heard our neighbor's wagon comin'. He was goin' to take us to the train and tend to the livestock while we were gone.

We loaded our rollin' trunk in the wagon and climbed in. Our neighbor set out for the train station in Chatham. Although it was the middle of the night, we were all wide awake and lookin' forward to our trip.

"I've got a feelin' this is a day we'll remember all the rest of our lives," said Carrie.

When we reached the station, we unloaded our trunk and stood on the train platform. It seemed to take the train forever to come. Finally, we saw its bright light around the bend. The conductor helped us get on the train. He swung his lantern to give the "All Aboard" signal.

We moved a lot faster on that train goin' back to Windsor than when we did comin' from Windsor a few years earlier.

Carrie and I slept until we jerked to a stop in Windsor. It was about the same time of mornin' it had been when we'd passed through Windsor on our way to Buxton four years ago. The sky was still dark as the train conductor called, "Windsor. Windsor is our next stop."

We got off the train and rolled our trunk down the platform to a waitin' livery. The lantern lights on the coach seemed to beckon to us. The driver was in his seat high above the lanterns, ready to take us wherever we wanted to go.

Uncle Edward walked on ahead of the rest of our little group. He was the one who knew about Amherstburg, so he called up to the driver, "Good mornin'. Can you take us to the dock where you get the boat to Amherstburg?"

"Good mornin'," said the driver. "Yes, I can take you."

"Carrie, did you hear that man's voice?" I whispered.

"Yes, what about it?"

"It sounded like our daddy's voice."

"Oh, Luther, you're dreamin'."

"No, I'm not! I think that's really Daddy."

"But that man has white hair and a beard. And Daddy's not even in Windsor. You're still asleep. Wake up."

Once we were beside the coach, we could look up into the driver's face. Carrie and I gasped.

Carrie said, "It *is* Daddy!"

For the first time in my life I was free to yell out loud: "DADDY! DADDY, it's us—Luther and Carrie!"

Daddy almost tumbled off the driver's seat. He tried to climb down to the ground while we tried to clamor up the side of the coach to where he was. We all met in a big three-way hug in midair.

For a long moment we were speechless. Finally, in amazement, Daddy touched our faces and whispered softly, "Luther and Carrie. I found my children after all these years. Thank God."

The sun was comin' up and we could get a better look at each other. All of us were boohooin' like babies. Daddy looked much older than when we'd split up in the winter of 1855. It wasn't only that his hair was white and he had a beard. He had deep wrinkles on his brow and he looked just plain tired.

Carrie and I had changed, too, but we'd been around each other while the changes had taken place little by little. I didn't realize how different we looked since Daddy'd last seen us.

Daddy climbed back up on the driver's seat and motioned to us. "Come on up here with me." As we did, he looked at us, sayin', "My gracious, I can't get over how much my children have grown. Look at you, Luther, you're quite a young man now. And, Carrie, you're quite a young lady."

Tears gushed from Daddy's eyes when he said, "I'm *so* happy to find you and proud to see what fine young people you grew to be. But I feel so bad not to have been with you to see you grow up." He was huggin' us all the time he was talkin'.

Uncle Edward and Aunt Christina had been standin' at the side of the coach since I'd yelled, "DADDY!" They wanted to give us a chance to talk

to him alone. After awhile, Uncle Edward cleared his throat.

Rememberin' his manners, Daddy told Uncle Edward, "I'm sorry. I forgot all about you wantin' a livery, sir . . . I just found my long-lost children and I forgot about everything else."

Uncle Edward said, "That's quite all right. We have lived for this moment."

Daddy scratched his head, wonderin' what Uncle Edward meant. Why would a stranger say that?

Aunt Christina stood there sobbin' without a sound. She was tremblin' like a leaf. When Uncle Edward spoke she couldn't hold back any longer. She blurted out Daddy's name, "Harvey Lee, I'm your wife's sister, Christina—from Virginia. We met up with your children in Detroit and have been searchin' for you and Emma ever since."

Daddy seemed to almost crumple on the driver's seat. Just as quickly, he leaned forward and asked, "You mean Carrie and Luther got to grow up around some kinfolk after all?"

"Yes. The children were travelin' alone. We met them when we were all at an Underground Railroad church in Detroit. The reason they came and sat by me was 'cause I reminded them of their mama."

Daddy said, "Oh, thank goodness! You don't know how many nights Emma and I have lain awake wonderin' whatever became of our children, and all the time they were in good hands. Thank goodness."

Then rememberin' Uncle Edward again, Daddy said, "I know you wanted me to take you down to the dock, but please let me take you by the house to see Emma. Seein' you all will do her a world of good. . . . Climb in the coach. This buggy ride is free!"

Carrie, Aunt Christina, Uncle Edward, and I climbed in and were talkin' and askin' Daddy questions as fast as his horse could gallop through the streets of Windsor.

Carrie asked, "Daddy how *is* Mama and . . . ?"

Daddy slowed the horse down to a pace and answered, "Not so well. She's been mopin' around and half sick ever since Dilly died and we lost track of you two."

I tugged at Daddy's shoulder and asked, "Daddy, did you say Dilly *died?*"

"Yes . . ."

"How? What happened, Daddy? Dilly was just a baby!"

"It was so awful. You remember how we were all put in different wagons when we got to that sawmill in Quincy?"

"Yes."

"Well, Mama and Dilly and I were put on a train in a boxcar. We were 'sposed to be goin' to Chicago.

We would have had enough food and water if the train had kept goin', but somehow our boxcar got left on a side track for eight long days."

"And you ran out of food?" I asked.

"Worse than that. Dilly was sick and we couldn't do nothin' for her."

"I remember Mama felt Dilly's head to see if she had a fever while we were hidin' from those slave catchers longside the Mississippi River," said Carrie.

"I remember that, too," I added. "Dilly yelled and Mama put a sugar tit in her mouth to get her quiet."

"Well, Dilly really was sick. It was just awful. If only we could have got out of that boxcar, Mama could have picked some wild herbs to nurse Dilly with. But we couldn't open the boxcar from the inside. We were trapped. Mama and I sat up night and day and held the baby, but there wasn't nothin' we could do."

"That's a shame," said Carrie. "Dilly was just startin' her life. She should have had a chance to be free."

I was in tears thinkin', The only freedom Dilly ever had was that day she ran away from me and led us to that stream.

Aunt Christina changed the subject back to Mama. She asked Daddy, "Do you think it will be too much of a shock for Emma when we all walk in?"

"No, indeed," said Daddy. "This is the best thing that could happen. She has been heartbroken, knowin' all the dangers we went through to escape, then losin' the children. She's asked me a million times, 'Was freedom worth the sacrifice?' "

We rounded the corner, and Daddy stopped the coach in front of a little cottage. He hitched up the horse and told us, "Wait here a minute." Even though his face and hair made him look old, he ran into the house like a little child.

We sat in the coach wonderin' what to expect.

CHAPTER

19

Pretty soon Daddy came to the front door with Mama. We'd thought Daddy had aged, but Mama looked at least ten years older than him. She was bent over and kind of lame. Her hair was gray and it was hangin' in wisps around her face. But the most hurtin' thing was the sad, sad look in Mama's eyes.

She stood in the door and squinted to see out. We could tell she couldn't believe the news when Daddy told her he had found us.

We couldn't wait any longer. Carrie, Aunt Christina, and I climbed out of the coach. We ran up to the door, each of us tellin' Mama who we were.

"Hello, Mama, it's me, Luther."

"Good mornin', Mama, it's me, Carrie."

"And, Emma, I'm your big sister, Christina."

Seein' us and hearin' our voices, Mama realized it *really* was us. She ran up to each of us.

When she came to me, she took her two hands and gently held my face between them. She kissed me on the forehead and hugged me tight. She did the same with Carrie and Aunt Christina. Then she said, "Oh, you can't know how I have dreamed the day would come when we could see each other again. I'd all but given up . . ."

"We had too, Mama," Carrie said.

"We thought we'd never find you again," I mumbled.

"And I sure never thought I'd see you after you left Virginia," said Aunt Christina.

Daddy stepped out the front door. "But we're all back together now!"

Uncle Edward had lifted our trunk on wheels out of the coach and was rollin' it toward where we were standin'. Aunt Christina introduced him to Mama and looked down at the trunk. "Emma, we've got a trunkload of food here. Can we bring it in? We've been on the way a long time, and I'm sure we could all use a bite to eat."

Mama smiled. (Later, Daddy told us it was the first time she had smiled in months.) "Please do come on in," she said. It looked like energy came

back into her body as she spoke. She turned to Aunt Christina. "I guess you thought I'd forgot my home trainin'." The two sisters hugged each other and laughed.

Mama made a big pot of coffee and we sat down to the happiest breakfast ever. We talked and laughed for hours. Finally, Daddy said to Uncle Edward, "We'd better get goin' if you still want to catch a boat to Amherstburg." As he spoke Mama pulled the wisps of hair back from her face.

Uncle Edward told Daddy, "We don't need to go anywhere. We were goin' to Emancipation Day in Amherstburg hopin' to cheer ourselves up. Findin' you and Emma is a hundred times better."

"Let me pour some more coffee," said Mama. "I know this is the best thing that's happened to Harvey Lee and me since we came to Windsor."

"Speakin' of Windsor," asked Carrie, "how'd you-all happen to move here instead of London? We looked high and low for you there."

"We took a ship from Chicago to Windsor," explained Daddy. "We met another runaway on board. We struck up a friendship and when he got to talkin', he told me his brother owned a livery stable in Windsor. He was a wheelwright and was comin' to Windsor to work with his brother. He thought with my horse trainin', his brother would hire me. I talked it over with your mama. We knew you thought we'd be in London so we went there first, but I couldn't find work."

Mama added, "We figured your daddy would be smart to come back and take the job in Windsor. It was a sure thing so we thought we'd take a chance on stayin' here. Daddy couldn't be sure of ever findin' work in London."

"Anyway, I knew I'd enjoy workin' 'longside the man who told me about his brother's livery stable," said Daddy.

Mama sat up straight and took Daddy's hand. "Your daddy *owns* that livery now. Those two brothers decided to move to Toronto and Daddy bought 'em out."

"How's business?" asked Uncle Edward.

"Very good," said Daddy. "I have some good drivers. But since I still enjoy horses and drivin', I take the early-mornin' shift. That way I can spend time with Emma durin' the day. The shop's right down the street. We call it the Freeman Family Library."

"*Freeman* family," said Luther.

Carrie added, "Why Freeman?"

"I forgot to tell you," said Daddy. "We changed our name from Lawson to Freeman when we moved back to Windsor. We thought it would make it harder for slave catchers to find us. But to get back to your question about business, Edward, it's pretty good. My only problem is we got so much business I need a full-time blacksmith."

"Maybe I can help you solve that problem," said Uncle Edward. "I'm a blacksmith. And after this past year I'm about ready to give up farmin'."

Daddy stood up, he was so excited. "Would you give some thought to comin' here and workin' with me?"

"Yes, I think I'd like that," said Uncle Edward. "Maybe we can rent out the farm and find a place to live close by here."

Aunt Christina winked at Mom. "You know I'd love that."

"Carrie and I would, too!" I yelled.

Carrie turned to our aunt. "We'd like to live with Mama and Daddy, if it's all right with you and them," she said.

"Of course you should," said Aunt Christina.

"That would be a dream come true," said Daddy, "for your mama and me to see you finish growin' up."

"We can try to make up for all the years we couldn't be together," said Carrie.

"Oh, yes! That would be wonderful!" said Mama. She looked ten years younger than when she had stood at the front door earlier that mornin'.

I thought about the way Emancipation Day had turned out for us. "Girl," I said to Carrie, "you *sure* were right this mornin' when you sat up in that wagon and said, 'I've got a feelin' this is a day we'll remember all the rest of our lives.' "

Mama, Daddy, Aunt Christina, Uncle Edward, Carrie, and I all laughed to our heart's content. We felt happier and freer than we had ever felt before.

Epilogue

Great-grandpa Luther held the mramnuo up so it sparkled in the sunlight. Then he tapped his ebony walking stick on the ground and leaned back in his cane chair. He had enjoyed telling about his adventures as much as his great-grandchildren had enjoyed hearing them. He knew at 101 years old he wouldn't always be around to tell the family story. But he had made sure that his great-grandchildren knew the story so they could tell their children. He hoped they'd always gather under his apple tree to share it.

Author's Note

This book gave you a glimpse of the turbulent times that preceded the Civil War. Social, political, and economic turmoil affected the entire nation and every individual in it. The institution of slavery was the crux of the conflict. It was viewed from at least four different perspectives:

—enslaved Africans who were bound for life to work without pay, and to be continually subject to sale and permanent separation from families and friends

—slaveholders who benefited from the products and services produced by slave labor

—abolitionists, both black and white, who were motivated for religious, political, or personal reasons

—proslavery sympathizers who, because of social or economic reasons, empathized with slave-holders

Collision between opposing forces was inevitable. There were frequent local conflicts that gained momentum and scope.

In both the South and the North, unrest had peaked in the late 1830s and 1840s when many antislavery societies were formed. The situation was made more critical by the passage of the 1850 Fugitive Slave Law. It was extremely hard on escaping slaves and abolitionists and provided, among other punishments, that "friends" working in the Underground Railroad could be fined $1,000 or imprisoned for six months if they were convicted of transporting or harboring slaves.

Slavery was not limited to the Deep South. There was slavery also in the New England and mid-Atlantic states, including New York, New Jersey, and Pennsylvania. These Northern states abolished slavery within their borders between 1777 and the early 1800s. The Missouri Compromise of 1820 allowed Missouri to enter the Union as a slave state. The Kansas-Nebraska Act of 1854 allowed Kansas and Nebraska to enter the Union without slavery restrictions.

During the fall and winter of 1855–1856 a little known but far-reaching conflict was raging on the Missouri-Kansas border. This was three years after

Harriet Beecher Stowe wrote *Uncle Tom's Cabin*, the book that dramatized the misery of slavery. It was a year before the Dred Scott decision in which the U.S. Supreme Court ruled that a slave who was taken to a free state or territory did not become free, and it was five years before the Civil War. No one knew what to expect.

From the earliest days, slaves had been escaping, sometimes with and sometimes without help from free black, white, and native American people who opposed slavery. The efforts that were made to aid fugitives were referred to as the "Underground Railroad." Actually, it was neither underground nor a railroad. It was called "underground" because it was secretive. It was against the law to harbor escaped slaves. It was referred to as a "railroad" because the mid-1800s was the period when real railroads had caught the imagination of the nation. Railroad terms were used as code names. For example, a "station" was a stopping place; a "passenger" an escaping slave; a "conductor" an abolitionist taking passengers from one station to another.

The Underground Railroad operated to some extent in more than thirty states and territories. In May 1859, Canada, Mexico, and the Caribbean were end points. At John Brown's convention in Chatham, Ontario, plans were made also to make Kansas a terminus of the Underground Railroad.

In this story, I introduced a fictional family whose adventures took place within the context of actual historical occurrences. However, there were instances when I employed artistic license to facilitate the telling of the story. For example, I altered the dates of the activities of two historical figures in Illinois, Professor David Nelson and Alan Pinkerton. In actuality, Dr. David Nelson operated Mission Institute and his Underground Railroad station in Quincy, and Alan Pinkerton and his family moved from Dundee to Chicago *before* 1855–1856. However, the roles I had them play in the story were consistent with things they did in real life.

I could find no records indicating whether or not William Lambert arranged for wagon drivers to meet former slaves at the Canadian border, but knowing the careful and detailed plans he and other members of the African American Mysteries secret society made for former slaves to live in Canada, it is conceivable that he did.

Like countless other enslaved Africans, Carrie and Luther's family escaped on the Underground Railroad with a dream of being able to benefit from their own labor, to get an education, and to exercise the right to vote. They met new challenges in freedom. Many other enslaved Africans never had an opportunity to be free.